Surrender's Passion

A Futuristic Erotic Romance

Aedan Sayla

Origins of Love Company

Publisher

Copyright © 2021 by Aedan Sayla

All rights reserved. No part of this publication may be reproduced, distributed or transmitted in any form or by any means, without prior written permission.

Publisher's Note: This is a work of fiction. Names, characters, places, and incidents are a product of the author's imagination. Locales and public names are sometimes used for atmospheric purposes. Any resemblance to actual people, living or dead, or to businesses, companies, events, institutions, or locales is completely coincidental.

Book Layout © 2017 BookDesignTemplates.com

Cover Art by Aedan Sayla

Aedan's books are available at: Amazon.com – Apple Books - Smashwords – Barnes & Noble – Kobo – Google Play Books – ebooks.com

Goodreads Page: Aedan Sayla

Author's Website: www.origins-of-love.org

Aedan Sayla's Blog – Musings: https://origins-of-love.org/musings

Author Contact Info: author-aedan-sayla@proton.me

Surrender's Passion / Aedan Sayla

Aedan Sayla

The Book List

(List last edited - 1/13/2023)

The Warriors of Mora Series

Book 1: *Submission of a Lady*
Book 2: *Warrioress Taming*
Book 3: *A Claimed Queen*
Book 4: *Possessing all of a Lady, Coming Soon*
Book 5: *The Unexpected Pleasure of a Slave, Coming Soon*

Apocalypto Series

Book 1: *A Drive to be Remembered*
Book 2: *Peril without Mercy*
Book 3: *The Will to Thrive, Coming Soon*

The Agents Series

Book 1: *Agent in Training*
Book 2: *Finding an Agent, Coming Soon*

Escaping Babylon Series

Book 1: *Foreign Princess, Coming Soon*
Book 2: *Queen in Hiding, Coming Soon*

The Badlands Series

Book 1: *The Baron Killer, Coming Soon*
Book 2: *The Cold Killers, Coming Soon*

American Apocalypse Series

Book 1: *City - Prison Land, Coming Soon*
Book 2: *Forest - Freedom Land, Coming Soon*

Standalone Books

Book: *The Huntsman*
Book: *Man on Fire*
Book: *A Russian Rose*
Book: *Tomorrow's Woman*
Book: *A Lady's Worth*
Book: *Charity's Gunman*
Book: *A Rebel's Persuasion*
Book: *Book Mate*
Book: *Brides of War*
Book: *Broken but Undefeated*
Book: *Cave Man*
Book: *Surrender's Passion*
Book: *The Forbidden Zone*
Book: *The Slave Princess, Coming Soon*
Book: *Lost, Coming Soon*
Book: *The Last Incan, Coming Soon*
Book: *His - Beauty in the Dark, Coming Soon*

Dedicated – To the preservation of true Biblical masculinity. In a world increasingly run by out of control feminist agendas, there is increasingly a lack of true masculinity to be found within the male population that increasingly is witnessing a decline in overall fitness of body, mind and spirit. This book is for men and women who appreciate true gender roles as they were created by God to be and even so this book will surely offend those who no longer want a man to be what he should be and think a woman should be almost anything apart from what she was created to be. *Sincerely, Aedan Sayla*

I Corinthians 9:19 – 23

19 - Although I am a free man and not anyone's slave, I have made myself a slave to everyone, in order to win more people.
20 - To the Jews I became like a Jew, to win Jews; to those under the law, like one under the law — though I myself am not under the law — to win those under the law.
21 - To those who are without that law, like one without the law — not being without God's law but within Christ's law — to win those without the law.
22 - To the weak I became weak, in order to win the weak. I have become all things to all people, so that I may by every possible means save some.
23 - Now I do all this because of the Gospel, so I may become a partner in its benefits.

— Source: HOLMAN BIBLE TRANSLATION

Content Warning

Dear reader, if per chance you did not see otherwise – this is a work of erotic fiction. The erotic content is quite vividly portrayed.

All primary sexual relations that take place are of a heterosexual standard and the age of the characters involved is 18+.

There are several scenes of 'sci-fi' violence. There are also elements of non-consent within the story.

The appropriate reading age is 18+.

CONTENTS

CHAPTER ONE

The Order of the Day

Brett closed her eyes tiredly, another day another mission. The orders were always the same.

Kill, kill, and kill.

Opening her eyes she glanced down at her hands and flexed her fingers. She was quite good at killing.

Actually she was very good and that was why at the ripe old age of 22 she had been given her own squad to lead. She had a way of finding the enemy and when she did it was lights out.

To date they put her active kill status at 213, but it was actually much higher than that.

"Are we there yet or what?" Groused out one of her underling squad members, a blonde with a very surly disposition.

Meeting her gaze Brett let her eyes bore into the other girls with all the intensity that she had become famous for and within moments the would be tough guy blinked and looked away from her.

The silent victory gained Brett closed her eyes again and shook her head as she mused over the phrase of speech, '*tough guy*'.

It was actually quite hard to get rid of everything of the masculine nature that had at one time dominated society. They were close to it though, but still things like this phrase of speech persisted even in a world now dominated by females.

Each mission saw them that much closer to realizing the goal of the high command, which was simple, the complete eradication of every last male human on earth.

The coming 24th century was going to be a girl's only world.

Without men all the problems of war and violence would be no more. When the last male fell there would be peace, which begged the question, what in this future utopia was she going to do?

All she knew, indeed all that she was good at, was fighting.

In the background she could hear the would be tough girl from the prior moment mumbling as she sought to cover over her momentary lack of dominance, "She's not really committed to the movement, look she doesn't even take the injections! She's simply a pleasure girl that knows some moves is all. She shouldn't be the one leading us."

Brett debated on whether to make an example of the girl or not and chose to refrain from doing so for the moment as some problems had a way of weeding themselves out. She knew that she was an exception to the norm for being part of the warrior class and not taking the standard injections.

Standard protocol injections for warrior class members was a heady dose of primarily testosterone along with mood stabilizers to counter the effects. In Brett's opinion all it did was make your muscles bigger and one slower.

For her speed was everything. Her quick reflexes had saved her more than once.

What need did she have to look like a boy anyway when the goal was to eliminate everything male in the first place?

No, she did not understand the pushing of taking male hormones for all active military personnel.

It seemed counterproductive somehow. Why become like the enemy if the goal was to destroy them on behalf of how terrible they were?

She was of the last generation to have been live seeded into being. No longer did they even need males to reproduce the species.

Advanced cloning and protein synthesis technologies had rendered the need for a male completely obsolete. In a female dominated world men were fast becoming endangered.

All the breeder slaves had been put to the torch a year ago. Not one male existed anywhere among the seven cities.

The only place that any male survived yet in was in the outlands. Here in the forest and plains of the outer wildlands they yet roamed, but even there they were increasingly fewer in number.

That said only kill squads like hers dared to come out here. It wasn't just the surviving men that were a threat in these outlands.

Beneath the transport ship taking them to their mission location within the shadowed confines of the forest and tall marsh grasses, life was a living hell. Literally hell on earth and in many ways the women of her time were directly responsible for it.

They had caused the extreme danger to exist by releasing prehistoric monsters brought back by genetic tampering. The purpose of the experimentation had been to supply a literal man eating force at work 24 hours a day all year long.

It had worked at first to some extent. The few remaining settlements of men had vanished, but then the monsters one by one had rebelled and resisted against the neural programming commands wired in to them and once that had occurred something else unexpected happened.

They started mating even though they had all been programmed to be born female. Their numbers grew and they soon hunted women with the same fervor as they did everything else.

Women might control the cities and the skies but the beasts held sway in the wilds and yet somehow men continued to survive. Although there were fewer of them to be sure, the ones that were left had become peerless fighters honed by the realities of simply surviving out here on the knife's edge of existence.

Their prowess at fighting was why it took whole squads such as hers to tackle one or two of them at a time. The surviving men were called Westwilds.

When driven the hardest they always tended to run to the West into an area of harsh forested terrain so insanely wild that no kill squads dared to venture on foot to it, because the monsters located there were even larger. The area was primarily avoided though because of electromagnetic anomalies left over from the wars of the past, anomalies that interfered with hover craft systems to the point of causing them to malfunction and drop out of the sky.

Eventually the alliance of the seven cities would need to go there, if men were to be wiped out once and for all, so that the days of womankind could commence fully.

One of the copilots of the hover transport was calling to her from up forward and snapping out of her harness she headed up to hear what she had to say. The hover transport known as a Mankiller X4 abruptly sloughed sideways in the air and Brett was sent tumbling even as the copilot screamed out, "We're hit!"

Gripping a hold of a strap Brett raised her head and looking out the window she took in the reality that through the portside hatch she was witnessing the hovercraft's engine entirely wreathed in flames. The craft shuddered hard again and glancing across the cargo bay she witnessed the other engine get taken out as well.

In short order she felt the ship begin to glide downward as her squad members screamed in terror and fought to either get out of their safety harnesses or hang on to them for dear life as if they were the only security they possessed in life.

In the brief few seconds remaining before impact Brett's mind was overwhelmed with the reality of all that was behind what was occurring. Engine failure like this was what happened if you flew too close to the wildlands in the West.

Now it was happening here on the very doorsteps of the seven cities!

This was only supposed to have been a routine patrol over an already cleared out sector.

The Mankiller X4 sliced through the treetops and then it was crashing into the massive trunks of old growth trees.

It disintegrated apart into pieces. Brett held on for dear life but with a sharp jolt she lost her grip on the harness and went flying through the air.

Screaming wildly did no good and with an abrupt '*ummfff*' she connected with the ground and skipped across it for what felt like an eternity.

Finally she came to a stop up against the base of a tree.

Breathing shallowly she worked on recapturing focus and evaluating for sure if she was even alive or rather in some post death dream sequence. It simply hurt too much for her to be dead though.

Lifting her head her dulled senses were greeted to the sounds of forest birds and monkeys crying out loudly at the sudden disturbance caused by the crashing hovercraft. Looking around she saw the torn off cargo bay portion of the hovercraft about 200 feet away.

Both the need for survival along with the responsibilities of leadership had her fighting to get her way up to her feet. Even though she disliked most of her squad the responsibility to lead them in this their greatest hour of need was strong.

Taking a staggering step forward she saw roughly half of her squad stumble out the back of the open hatchway of what had once been a ship reflecting the best technology had to offer. Now it was simply a piece of chewed up metal cut into pieces.

Though bloody her squad members had their weapons up which was good. The monsters of the area were sure to be on the way with the explosions of the forward section now wreathed in flames serving as an attracting beacon for them.

Suddenly she had the feeling of being watched. No sooner did the sense of that occur to her then also came the instinct to duck off to the side.

Tumbling headfirst into the undergrowth she saw the bark get blown off the tree that had been directly ahead of her.

Fueled by the panic for survival Brett kept rolling and somersaulting back up to her feet she began dodging and running as more gunfire rang out.

Men! Men had done this?

Her squad looked about in consternation at the forest and yelling at the dunce heads Brett screamed, "Get down you idiots!"

One girl took a salvo to the chest and the rest of them scattered almost instantly, as they were shook out of the shock of the harsh landing, by the even harsher reality that they were under attack.

Usually it was always them hovering just above the treetops with them being the ones raining down hell on the running men below, but this time was clearly different.

For the most part the only time they actually landed and set foot in the forest was to confirm a positive takedown or finish off a wounded man that had managed to find somehow to hide himself from the eyes in the sky. The current scenario was something that they almost never trained for and Brett had warned her superiors of the lack in training, but no one had listened.

It was simply too easy of a search and kill approach to simply hover overhead and kill the men like shooting fish in a barrel than to go through the rigors of harder training of personnel and more active ground combat tactics.

Ducking past the streams of bullets being issued out by her own squad members in return fire upon the forest she made it the last of the distance to them.

Turning about she beheld nothing but the boles of trees and leafy understory growth. All they were doing was wasting ammo!

"Stop firing and fall into line now!" Brett screamed, as grabbing up a pack and her own weapon she headed for the other open end of the hovercraft section that had been torn off from the tail portion of the fuselage.

Reflecting the befuddlement of poor training along with shock only half of those remaining alive listened to the voice of her authority and gave up firing to follow after her, while the others elected to stay in the confines of familiarity and away from the wildness of the forest that surrounded on all sides.

Brett did not wait for them but bursting out the other side of the fuselage she ran hard into the cover of the trees. The five that had stayed behind realized almost instantly their mistake even as two rocklike items clattered to the floor at their feet.

They only had time to begin to scream before all life was taken from them as both improvised grenades exploded. Brett heard the blasts but didn't look back.

She focused her efforts on running and the five members of the squad that had followed her fought to keep up as each was fighting an inner war of hysteria and shock. Downed crews in the forest never made it back alive, for it was a well-known fact that the forest took no prisoners.

Running for over an hour straight Brett made it into a clearing that had a small brook running through it. Breathing heavy with hands pressed to her flared out hips she focused on regaining some measure of calm.

Stumbling into view the five straggling members of her squad lumbered into the clearing and casting their weapons aside they dove on to their knees beside the water and started lapping away at it like animals. Brett looked down upon them with utter disgust.

The injections they took may give them male like muscles and physiques, but in reality they had no conditioning at all. With so low of a body fat index they were prone to dehydrating quickly.

Again her past complaints to her superiors rang out loudly in her own ears.

Shaking her head she looked away from the sight of her useless crew filling themselves so full of water that they wouldn't be able to run without puking it all back up.

Her gaze landed on a pair of eyes that watched her with an intensity that to her was previously unimaginable. Through sheer course of training her hands moved fast as she fought to unsling her gun and bring it to bear, but as her wild flaring eyes took in more of the shadowy outline of the man before her she watched him raise a hand and snap his fingers.

In the slow-motion sequence of the moment the sound of the snap of his fingers was unbelievably loud sounding. All hell broke loose behind her as the forest echoed with the sound of both the roar of beasts unleashed and women caught unaware.

Gun up Brett wheeled around only to see no less than five raptors carving bloodily into the bodies of her screaming crew completely caught off guard beside the brook of running water now rapidly being stained red with their blood. They were past helping and in dawning horror for what felt like the worst threat of all she wheeled back around to face the man who with a snap of his fingers had set a new reality into motion.

That new startling reality was that man now controlled the monsters that had been brought back from the dead for the very purpose of eliminating him from the ecosystem. It was the unlikeliest of all alliances, but the reality of it was being proven in the moment just the same.

What kind of a man had the authority to exert control over as ferocious of a beast as those gathered behind her?

The man was still standing there calmly and as her eyes met his she took in the reality of something very dominantly powerful about him that instantly made her feel something that she had never felt before.

What this man had was what her commanders had invested everything into the pursuit of total annihilation of, but even so their best efforts had failed because if ever there was an alpha male it was this one, as just the power of his gaze was somehow mesmerizing in its effect upon her.

Her sense of control snapped apart into little pieces and instead of firing her gun she felt it fall from her limp fingers as every fiber of her being went into flight mode from something far more powerful than her.

Lunging to the side and away from the man saved her life as a raptor sprang upon the spot where she had just been standing. Its snapping jaws clamped down upon her falling rifle instead of the flesh they had yearned for the taste of.

Brett did not look back, but tore through the forest in the literal race of her life. She ran and ran for what felt hours, until she could tell that there was a clearing away of the forest up ahead.

She wasn't that far from her host city. Breath coming in shattered gasps she tore free of the last of the trees and out into the safety corridor grassland were no trees were allowed to grow so that a firing perimeter could be maintained around the city both day and night.

Running into the tall grass she expected to be torn up off her feet and devoured at any second, but the expected attack did not come. Instead she tripped and falling forward she landed hard.

Adrenaline driving her she found her way back up to her feet even as her lungs raged in need for air that simply wasn't there in great enough supply. Glancing back she saw him.

He was standing outlined on the ridge just at the edge of the forest with the entire posse of his monsters arrayed to either side of him waiting for his command to attack. No command came from him though.

A disturbance of sound from behind her made her look towards the city. The air was bristling with airships headed directly for her.

Glancing back to the forest she beheld that the man along with his monsters was gone.

He'd purposely let her escape!

But why?

Falling to her knees in exhaustion and fractured nerves Brett waited for the city force to arrive. As her body calmed down with its pursuit for air coming to a close she reflected on the new reality that had been revealed in this day.

Mankind had just declared war on them and try as she might, as she beheld more oafish bodied warriors fall in all around her with the false bravado brought on by countless easy winning escapades, she admitted privately to herself that they didn't have a chance against real men like the one that had just been hunting her.

It was over. Everything was over.

The level of hate that she'd seen in that man's eyes wouldn't rest until every last one of her kindred was dead and where there was one like him there were surely going to be more as well.

CHAPTER TWO

Beautiful Sky Hunter

Two Miles Away

I slid off the back of Mandy and with an affectionate birdlike twill she pushed her snout against my back and was then off running away with the rest of her brethren as the skies became thick with Mankillers x-raying the forest intent on finding heat signatures of any kind to blowup to kingdom come.

Approaching the cave entrance Tajic looked up from where he had been cleaning his rifle. Looking me over with a smirk he said, "You let her go didn't you my friend."

I didn't say anything, but went on to move past him.

"Ah, yes she was a fast one she was and no injections either. Pure female that one with that pair of wide hips and hot ass of hers to prove it."

I looked downward at him and immediately he lifted his hands away from me as if something about me had singed him and melodramatically he said, "I get it! No one talks about the chick with the hot ass but you my friend, but tell me, hot ass and everything else aside, why did you let her go? She's going to tell them everything she saw."

"Why does it matter if she does? Her commanders already know and have been sitting on the truth for months. That girl's story will hit the actual streets and fear will run rampant and fear my friend is an even more powerful ally than a kill squad of monsters at your command."

Nodding his head Tajic said, "I see the wisdom in doing that. So when we take the city down full of fearful boygirls do you mind if I separate the all-girl chick out from the pack for myself?"

I raised a hand as if to hit him and Tajic leaned away laughing, "I get it Ranvold. She's yours. No one will get between you and the hot girl with the sweet ass from the city. Maybe having her to play with will make you nicer to the rest of your friends. I certainly hope so anyway as you are a bit too dialed in these days."

I looked away. Not wanting to admit the truth, but the truth was undeniable.

Speaking softer Tajic said, "It's been three years since that bomb took Marie and your baby away from you. It's okay to admit to the fact that you saw something today that you wanted as a man."

With aggravation I glanced back to Tajic. The man had a mouth that wouldn't shut up, but he was my friend and briefly I nodded and said, "Now get your butt inside before they pencil us out for good."

"Okay boss, but I know it is not my butt you are thinking of."

I made to hit him, but he dodged out of the way and in the darkness of the cave I smiled briefly, because he was right. It wasn't his butt at all that I was thinking about.

The girl had simply been different, maybe chiefly because she still looked like one. Separating her out of the herd wouldn't be easy though.

Breaking her spirit to do my will would be harder still, but that said I did have some experience in the matter.

Marie had been a Sky Hunter. Right up to the day she had caught more than she could handle.

It had taken a while, but she'd come to love and serve me like only a man could wish for. It was painful to think of what we'd had with each other and how it was forever gone along with the future of our child.

The girl from today reminded me of Marie and yet she was different. More experienced and harder, but no less beautiful of form.

She'd break. It might come hard for her, but she'd break and when she did I'd fill her full of my cock and go about seeding the life of another child within her womb and then after that another and another until I once again had the future that I'd lost in the past.

A family that would never have to live in the fear brought on by the offbeat controlling machinations of a feminist driven culture gone to the extreme.

I would see to that, even if it meant giving my life in order to make it possible for mankind to once more live freely upon the face of the earth again.

CHAPTER THREE

Crucified

Brett glanced back and forth along the row of superior commanders. Not one of them had batted an eye throughout the duration of her report.

She simply couldn't believe it! Didn't they realize the gravity of the situation?

Didn't they…… they did!

Brett could see it now, the fear they were trying so hard to mask behind looks of impartiality. They'd already known everything that she'd had to report about.

Somehow they had already known.

Speaking softly Brett stated to the room in general, "You already knew all this though didn't you. You know man has gained an advantage over us by enlisting the monsters to his side."

Several of the commanders glanced among themselves and then finally one in seniority said, "Go ahead and tell her."

A lesser ranking commander spoke into the stillness, "We lost contact with Elliamsa two weeks ago. There's been no word from them at all. We sent out a scout ship. She didn't come back. We sent out a squad. They only got close enough to see that the city was destroyed and were able to relay it to us over the radio before they too were destroyed. Men have found a way to render our hovercraft obsolete as it were."

Brett stared in shock at the group. Elliamsa was the second largest of the cities of women and the closest to the west lands. Her own city was the next closest.

The city of Vtarga was only 90 miles by air from Elliamsa and here these commanders sat letting the populace of the city completely clueless as to what was going on!

Wetting her dry lips Brett asked, "If you knew our craft had become rendered useless why send us out on a reconnaissance mission knowing they had the ability to bring us down?"

The group remained silent. The answer was simple enough to be realized though.

She and her squad had been set up to act as bait to test out the new found capabilities of the Westwilds. With that in mind Brett concluded the reality, as she had previously wondered about, as to the quick response of force from the city being a bit too quick.

Even then the response had been entirely bungled, with no enemy contacts found within miles of the city. What did that say about the level of preparedness their armed forces could boast?

Cold fingers squeezed about her heart as she took in the reality of how little she mattered to these leaders of the people.

One of her commanders looking her over disdainfully said, "Well, you did at least manage to survive. That's the first for a downed in the forest hovercraft crewman anyway."

A fellow officer gave the speaker a sideways glance and the speaker quickly corrected, "I mean crew woman of course."

Brett felt like screaming. A whole city had been annihilated and these puffed up loony birds were bickering over word semantics!

Doing her best to reign in her emotions she asked, "What are we going to do?"

"Only one thing to be done. We need to invade the outlands to the West at once and destroy whatever weapon they've devised that interferes and takes out our hovercraft. It will be risky, but once we have the skies back we'll blow them all to hell once and for all."

Brett stared blankly at the woman, who was the person in charge of her people in time of war, before asking with incredulousity, "And how are you going to get there?"

"Why by marching. How else? The skies are clearly shut off to us for now. Your experience today proves it."

Brett stared about wildly as she felt a rising tide of emotion swell out of all control within her. Expressing her emotions loudly she said, "You are going to get us all bloody killed if you do that!"

"You had best keep that tongue of yours in check squad commander, others have suffered extreme disciplinary treatments for far less. As it is you're walking on thin ice for blabbing away about the fortitude of men and monsters being at their beck and call on your way into this committee briefing."

"I said nothing but the truth!"

"That's enough! We as a committee are not interested in the truth! It is our job to see that control is enforced so that order can be maintained. As an agent of the Armed Forces we expect more from one such as your rank, but all we see coming out of you is the sniveling emotions befit of the status of a pleasure girl. You even look like one!"

Every one of the bordering leaders of defense nodded their heads in agreement with the primary committee member's words. Brett was struck in the moment by how utterly clueless they all were of reality.

This city was doomed for extinction. Indeed so were women, if women could be called what was in front of her.

In a way Brett wasn't sure that they were as she felt no identity with them as a woman. Come to think of it the few friends that she did have were all pleasure girls.

Girls, who were kept off the injections so they kept their female form and mannerisms which made them more desirable to the growing number of she-males within the population.

Brett shook her head and said, "Do whatever you want then, but I'm not going to fight any more for the likes of this society. I've never openly questioned the motives behind our movement, but now as I look at you studded out popping jays I can see I was wrong to blindly trust everything that I have in regards to the elimination of men from our species as being a good thing. In seeking to eliminate them from our society, a society that has produced the likes of you idiots along with all the souless hunk brained morons I've had to fight alongside these past few years, it has truly become something more despicable than what we've been trying to eliminate. We have no order or balance as a culture. We as a whole are unnatural even as all of our new generational offspring are currently being unnaturally derived. Mark my words, for in my travels to the forest I have seen a law of nature in action, which is that everything that is unnatural will be weeded out and summarily destroyed with time. I've wondered about this natural law for some time only to now see that it is true. Not one of our cities will remain and indeed they shouldn't. We doomed ourselves by our own self-imposed excessiveness and to my utter shame I reflect now on how I've had such a large part in doing what I now know and yes, maybe what I've known all along, is terribly wrong."

Silence reigned in the room as Brett met the glare of her military's overseers, who as one looked like they wanted to consumer her whole. The veracity of their hate for her was sickening to behold.

Had she been like this previously?

Oh God, she surely must have been to have so senselessly hunted down as many men as she had.

How and why everything was suddenly coming to matter in a spiritual way was beyond her to even comprehend in the moment. Who was God even?

Whoever He may be He must surely hate her!

Brought back to the reality of the moment by the lead committee member's voice she heard her say, "Guards, take this traitor out and crucify her."

Brett was seized a hold of and with fear she heard the committee member add with deep satisfaction, "And see that it is done upside down."

Tears coursed out of Brett's eyes as she was drug away. Crucifica-tion was bad enough of a way to go, but upside down only made it worse.

She'd seen it done to men in the past. Eventually their heads ex-ploded because of the blood not flowing to the extremities as it should.

It was a terrible way to go, but in a way she deserved it.

Knowing the truth of that though didn't make it any easier to have to face though.

CHAPTER FOUR

Unwelcome Rescue

Tajic gazed through the glasses at the city in the late afternoon sunlight. Its architecture lacked allure.

Indeed as a whole it appeared to be both grey and dull. Soon it would be in flames and the grayness replaced with the charring blackness of soot.

Something with color caught his eyes and focusing the glasses he abruptly came away from the tree he was leaning against. He gazed only a moment longer in order to verify what he had seen before he was up and running back into the tunnel complex behind him.

Ranvold

I looked up as Tajic came to a sudden halt before me. He was breathing heavy.

He pointed back down the tunnel and said, "The girl, you know, the one you......"

"Get to it, Tajic!" I stated testily, not wanting him to go into details in front of my division commanders.

"They crucified her."

I stood up and so did the others and as a final nail in the coffin Tajic added, "Upside down."

Silence reigned heavy in the aftermath of Tajic's words.

Solanin spoke, "We could postpone the attack and mount a rescue operation instead."

I shook my head immediately '*no*'.

"Ranvold……Tajic talks a lot. We….. we know of your interest in the girl. It would be good for you to have a wife again. You've been different since Maria's death. We don't mind holding the attack off for another day."

I met Solanin's caring gaze, "I appreciate the sentiment, but no. Whether I like the girl or not it doesn't matter in terms of the importance of our overall success in this war for survival. We've worked too hard to survive in order to take any risks to our plan of action not succeeding now. That said, I do think we could move the attack up several hours without compromising anything. Maybe…. she should be able to survive till then."

My division commanders as one slapped a fist against their armor plated chests and with confidence Solanin said, "We will see to the changes. We attack an hour before sunset."

I nodded and then was left alone as they all quickly left to do their jobs. I made my way out to the cave opening and from there I stared out at the city on the plain beyond.

What had she done to tick her superiors off so badly as to have them do to her what they had done?

I didn't know for sure, but whatever it was, somehow it made the girl more intrinsically likable to me because of it.

Softly, I prayed aloud, "God please keep her alive."

"So be it." Came from close by.

I glanced to Tajic standing nearby.

Instead of hitting him for being such a loud mouth I reached out and squeezed his shoulder with appreciation. Attacking at sunset instead of tomorrow morning would give me a chance at saving her, where it wouldn't have been a likely reality in the early hours of dawn.

By morning she would most likely have gone the way of so many men tortured in the past by the women of the cities.

~~~~~~~~~

Her whole body trembling Brett hung helplessly upside down. The pain in her head was unbearable.

A trickle of blood had begun to seep out of her nostrils and it was only a matter of time before her eardrums blew out.

Crying did no good, but it was all she could do because of the pain that she was in.

Breathing was especially hard. She could no longer feel her feet and her hands stretched out to either side of her throbbed with the pain of too much blood.

In order to breathe her lungs had to literally lift her whole body and it was only a matter of time before her oxygen depleted system collapsed and her heart exploded. Indeed it was a race, her head or her heart, which would explode first.

The worst thing of all was there simply was no hope. No one was going to save her from this.

Dimly her eyes opened as noise beyond the beat of her heart and the rasp for each breath came to her. There was fire and thunder and yet the thunder wasn't from the sky surely as there was no storm.

She could see that much at least in the twilight that was falling upon the land. No the thunder was from the hordes of monsters she could see rampaging over the city's walls and gateways.

Bitterly she acknowledged that she didn't need to worry about her head or her heart failing first, as soon she would be eaten down whole like a staked out goat.

Something happened at her hand and then the other one and then she felt her body moving.

She was flat. Breathing in deeply she convulsed on the ground as the blood went pouring out to her extremities again.
~~~~~~~~~

All of her deadened nerves woke up and she cried out with pain even as her body demanded heavy breathing from her to make up for the lack of air she'd had for hours on end.

Coming back to life was painful as intrinsically she'd known she was near to death. Laying in complete exhaustion upon the ground as it felt like her heart was about to burst anyway she nonetheless took in the sensory experience of feeling a pair of big hands squeezing down the length of her arms and legs making the blood flow once more out to where it should.

Wearily Brett's eyes opened and there she saw him hovering just over her. The man from the forest.

Swallowing she managed to croak out, "Why?"

Gazing down into her eyes he said with a deep voice that made tingles radiate throughout her flesh, "Because I want you."

Already trembling Brett shivered all the more upon hearing his words. Oh God, out of the frying pan and into the fire!

Weakly her arms rose up to push against him as she said, "No!"

His hand moved to the side of her neck and pressed and unconsciousness quickly began beckoning to her senses. In alarm she gazed up at him as her whole body was drug down into sleep.

A sleep she knew would end only to be soon followed by this man's possession of her. She shook her head weakly, but staring down into her eyes enigmatically he said, "Fight all you want to, but soon enough you will call me Master and do whatever I command you to."

Shaking Brett blinked and closed her eyes as the pressure of his finger drove her under into the realm of unconsciousness. An unconsciousness haunted with the nightmare vision that he was right.

She was no man's slave, but now....now she might just not have a choice.

~~~~~~~~~

"Dude, she's beautiful. I can see what drove you to want her so."
~~~~~~~~~

I glanced at Tajic and responded with, "She's more than just what is to be seen on the surface."

"Yeah, I can see that too. Solanin sent me to report, it's a complete wrap-up. All city defenses are busted up and there are only scattered pockets of resistance that should all be wrapped up by morning. Casualties have been minimal."

Nodding I stood up with my girl held in my arms.

As I started off for the forest I said, "Start putting this place to the torch."

"Yes, Sir!"

CHAPTER FIVE

A New Name

I watched her as her eyelids began to twitch. There was a flutter of eyelashes and then an opening of the eyes altogether.

They stared at the ceiling of my abode for several long moments then I watched as an abrupt shift of conscious awareness hit. She reared up off the table she was on and looked about wildly.

Seeing me sitting in a chair nearby she promptly fell off the far side of the table in her effort to be away from me. She hit the ground with an audible thump, but was back up on her feet in the next second.

Blinking rapidly she swayed about on her feet and I sensed she was on the verge of passing out, but with a steadying hand pressed up against her forehead she righted her focus and came back from the brink of unconsciousness.

Breathing heavy she looked at me in sheer panic driven hysteria. That was good.

It showed me that she respected me.

We stared at each other for several long moments and then with a gesture to the chair in front of me I said, "Come over here and sit down before you fall down."

She mutinously shook her head '*no*' and stayed where she was. She was beautiful even in the scattered disarray she was caught up in at the moment.

Softly, I spoke, "If you don't come to me then I will come to you. Your choice."

She swallowed and shakily she wiped at sudden beads of sweat on her forehead. She was in no condition to fight and she knew it.

Stiffly she came unglued from her position and advanced as warily as a cat expecting to flee at a moment's notice from the jaws of a larger predator.

Indolently I remained at rest all the while watching her come closer. She had courage, but even it had a breaking point.

She hesitated midstride and I could see that she had gone as far as her nerves would allow. Then, I watched as sudden tears came to her cheeks.

Aggressively she wiped at them as if angry that I had seen them.

She glanced at me once more and I said, "Sit down."

Her body shaking she made it the last few steps to the chair across from me and sat down all the while looking at me as if I was the stuff of nightmares untold. We were now but five feet apart from each other.

As she did her best to melt into the leather upholstery of the chair I idly commented out loud, "The Finisher."

"What?" She hoarsely croaked out in response.

"The name you've managed to acquire for yourself among the Westwilds over the past few years."

She blinked in apparent shock at what I had just said.

"Do you know how it came about you being called that?"

She shook her head '*no*', looking still very much afraid and yet slightly curious at the same moment.

"Because you always finished your hunts. I believe 317 of them to be exact. A very impressive statistic for just three years of service."

She looked down then and the emotion I saw reflected in her features wasn't fear so much as what I took to be shame instead. It was also clear that she expected some kind of revenge to be enacted upon her for what she'd done in the past.

In fact, in some ways it looked like she had been expecting it and was even in acceptance of it. All of this went to tell me that she still had a consciousness, which meant her soul was still intact.

"I respect you."

She looked up at me with astonishment clearly written across her face. It was very much not what she had expected to hear.

"I respect you, because you always handled yourself as a soldier. Most of the men you slew were outcasts, only a few were acquaintances and one was a friend."

The fear was back in her eyes again and with a voice that echoed of the sultry potential waiting to be unlocked in her she asked, "You respect me because I killed them?"

"No, I respect you because of how you killed them. You never took a prisoner back to the city to be tortured. Every time you shot to kill and if it was execution style you killed them quickly. In a culture such as the one you were raised in, that universally delights in the torment of injured or enslaved men, you are a notable exception to the norm. Don't get me wrong, I do not like what you have done in the past, but I can forgive it."

She stared at me in wonder and then blinking she looked away. I sat quietly as I gazed at the inner turmoil all my words had invoked within her.

"Why....why would you do that?"

Looking down at my clasped together hands I reflected for a moment before responding with, "Because once I was far worse than you. I killed both men and women indiscriminately and even to my shame - with pleasure at times. Anyone's life who got in the way of my survival was forfeit. I was utterly vicious and seemingly without any governing control other than for cruelty."

She drew up with an abrupt hitch of breath and glancing at her I saw her whisper out, "You're him! You're the leader of the resistance. The man they call Ranvold."

I smiled bittersweetly as I saw the expressed horror of a new conscious awareness worse than the first awaken and spread across every fiber of her being.

"I see that my reputation precedes me. Tell me, what do you know about me?"

"I....I ... what you said. You don't take prisoners. It was revealed in an interrogation years ago that you had begun a movement and then you dropped off the radar. We thought you were dead. The high command leveled 250 acres of forest where you were supposedly meeting with other Westwilds."

Nodding I said, "It was a close one. They almost got me. Tell me, to get such information out of a Westwild, as one trusted enough to know of our meeting taking place, what did they do to him?"

She bit her lip and looking away she whispered, "They crucified him...... upside down."

Nodding, I said nothing in response.

She looked back at me and I met her gaze.

Softly she whispered, "What are you going to do with me?"

"I told you the straight of it two days ago. I'm going to mate you as often and however I wish to. In the process of time should we be blessed with children we will have a family together, you and I. I may even come to love you one day. Of everything that may occur I have to admit that I'm not sure about the last one. I have loved someone before. In fact it was that love God used to change me. I captured a number of years ago now a girl from one of your cities. She was like you in some ways. I was on the verge of killing her, when I, mesmerized by her beauty found myself tying her up and mating her forcefully instead. I didn't stop. Days became weeks, weeks became months. A whole year went by. Her hate for me, my hate for her, somehow with time it changed into something else. I began to see a future. Not just one of survival but an actual future. A future worth fighting for. A future without all the senseless killing I had involved myself with just in order to survive. I started to talk about it with other men. The men of the Western lands began to listen as if hearing such words come from one such as I as simply being to earth shattering not to take notice of. Soon words became an idea and that idea of universal freedom began to unite us. We stopped killing each other in the pursuit to survive and started working with each other instead. It quickly became clear to all of us that we had stumbled into a better way of life. A way of life that we would never be allowed to live out peacefully as long as we were hunted from the air by the women of the cities. Many meetings took place as plans were agreed to and alliances formed. At one such scheduled meeting, Maria, that was her name, she was there with me. She was four months pregnant with our first child. The bombs fell. She died in my arms."

The girl before me in the chair looked away as if overcome by something.

Continuing to speak despite my reluctance in general to share anything about myself of a personal nature I said, "I could've gone either way at that moment. I could've descended once more into the insane fury of my past and become Ranvold, The Crusher, again with a list of kills to my name far exceeding your own, but I reflected that the misfortune that had befallen me and taken away a part of my heart that I didn't even know I still had was in some ways not something that hadn't been deserved. I was a cruel man and to some extent I remain that man today. The difference though is I asked the question, "*What is the point of life?*' and to my surprise God, Himself spoke to me. Already humbled, already broken by grief, I was perhaps in the most receptive place to hear from Him that I had ever been before in my life. I listened, I pondered, I asked questions, I read His words in the Bible, and with time I became a new man. Strangely I, for whatever reason, have always been a leader and many followed me down the path of discovery that I had embarked on in the spiritual, until it seemed that all of the tribes looked to me of all people for spiritual guidance. True irony if ever there was. Since then I've done my best to do right by all of them."

"By killing women?"

"No, by ending a war that should never have come to be. In order to have peace first there must be a war to eliminate what will never be at rest with those of us content to live in peace with one another. We would've let your cities of women alone and allowed you to rot out of existence in complete moral disjunction, but over and over it has been you the aggressor coming into our lands intent to destroy us. There can be no peace with something that can never be at peace with itself. Look at you, the essence of true womanhood and yet they crucified you. A snake biting its own tail. No, we will end this war and the cities of women will be no more along with all that they stood for in terms of ideology. The struggle then in the aftermath of war will be to not replicate the mistakes of the past that have led to this state of dysfunction within humanity."

She'd been staring at me intently as I talked and seeing words building up within her I paused and waited for her to speak them.

With emotional vigor they bubbled out of her full lips, "And who gives you the right to say a whole people should die?"

"I am man, I make a decision based on my discernment of what I think is right. As a woman of the cities are you going to defend what your brethren have done and have been about in regards to the sought out destruction of all men?"

She struggled for a moment to speak, but the answer was clearly '*no*' and she had no way to speak against the truth of it.

Softly I said, "In the same way neither am I excusable for how I once was and rightfully deserved to be put down as any mad dog should be. What I am currently about now is something entirely different. The extremes of hate that both men and women have been embroiled in for far too long against one another must stop. My goal is to bring them back together. If it has to be by force then it will be by force, if it can be done peacefully than it will be done by peace, but it will be done one way or another."

She was staring at me again and nervously she looked away.

Her jaw firmed and she looked back at me with as much bravado as she'd been able to muster yet so far, "So when do you forcefully make me come to heal like a dog in order to fulfill your togetherness goal for the species?"

"Any time I wish to."

I stood up and all the bravado fled from her eyes to be replaced with the look of a woman very much feeling that she was in extreme danger.

Despite her fear she said, "I will not submit to you. Taking me by force is not a submission on my part. It's simply rape."

Smiling I said, "I know and yet you will submit to me. In fact, I will see to it that you submit yourself to me in the most vulnerable of ways a woman can be known by a man. Mark my words you will do it of your own free will and stay obediently put as inch by inch my cock slides into your body until there is no more of it to go in."

She was shaking now and I could tell that the confidence of my words had made a deep impact upon her.

I turned away and made for the door.

Her words stopped me, "I'm not her."

I turned around and looking her up and down I said, "I assure you that I know that. You are not a replacement fantasy of a past that I can never revisit. Maria is gone. I can't change that. I can change how I progress into the future and you, my dear, Olivia, that is the only reason you're not tied down right now being mated by me to my heart's content. I very much want to have you. But I want to be a better man too and so I resist against my urges and in doing so I give you the respect of having more time than I ever gave to Maria. You have a lot to thank Maria for and no doubt so do I. Feel free to move about my house as you wish as in a way it is now your home as well. You can go outside, but do not go beyond the clearing or I will be deeply disappointed to return home and find the beautiful and vivacious creature that you are nothing more than a pile of dung and chewed up bones only fit to be spread out on my garden. I assure you that a future spent by being dominated by me as your mate has more to offer then being a tasty meal for one of my pets."

I opened the door.

"Where are you going?"

I looked back at her, "I have a war to finish before I can come home to the earned privilege of mastering you to my heart's content."

Her face paled and I could see that the hardness of my words were in echo to the fact that despite my efforts I was still a cruel man.

I didn't expect her to speak again, but she did. "The.... pleasure girls....you don't need to kill all of them. They....there little more than slaves to the others. I think...... I think some would even welcome life with a man if they were given the option."

Touched, I softly responded with, "We already took notice of that fact. We haven't been killing them, they, like you will serve as mates for the men of the Western lands."

"Thank you for that at least." She said softly before adding, "I won't be here when you return."

Smiling, I shut the door.

She had no idea.

Thinking better of it and realizing that it worked to my advantage in terms of breaking her to my will I reopened the door.

She stood up abruptly as if expecting me to suddenly ravish her.

Oh how I wished!

Instead I picked up a piece of chalk and drew a vertical dash on the stone wall of the house. Laying the chalk down on the table I said, "I will return in exactly 2 weeks. Today marks the first day of my absence Olivia. Best of luck in remaining alive in your attempts to escape before then."

"My name is not Olivia, its Brett!" She exclaimed back with in retort.

"I don't care whatever it was. Your mine now and I've named you Olivia and that is what you will be called from this day forth."

CHAPTER SIX

Two Weeks

Brett stared at the closed door and then the mark on the wall.

Two weeks.

Shakily she wiped at her forehead. Feeling exhausted suddenly she sat back down in the chair.

Two weeks was plenty of time to make an escape.

She didn't have to try this very second to mount a getaway, which was good, because crucifixion ordeal had not left her in a state of being able to handle that much.

She felt utterly worn out despite the fact that she had been sleeping for hours, actually days.

Glancing back to the door and around the spacious interior of the one roomed house she summed up her surroundings as being both warm and cozy.

The reality of finding it to be so was strange though. This place, indeed him, were nothing like she would have ever expected them to be.

Some part of her acknowledged that it would be nice to live in a place like this, this place actually.

Shaking her head she pulled away from the notion of such a thing, because to do so meant to surrender.

Surrender to a man - that she simply would never allow herself to do.

He may in the end rape her, but she would not submit of her own free will. No, she would not.

Anyway, she wouldn't be here upon his return and so it didn't really matter. She would rest today and focus on getting stronger.

Almost immediately upon that thought out resolution her stomach growled loudly. Hunger brought her back up to her feet.

Walking slowly she made her way into the side of the large room that resembled a kitchen. There were all the cooking implements one would expect to find in a well-stocked cooking area, even knives.

Picking a sturdy one up she tucked it away in her belt. What a fool he was!

There was already a fire simmering in the stove and something nearby it caught her eye. It was a dish with a clay cover on top of it that had a stream of steam escaping around the edges.

Lifting the lid she found a large portion of what looked like a mixture of vegetables, mushrooms and meat stewed together in an herby smelling thick broth. It smelled absolutely wonderful.

She picked the dish up and her eyes traced over as she did so to read the note that had been beneath the dish.

"May you enjoy. Have a good day Olivia."

"My name is Brett!" She said mutinously, even as she picked up a spoon and took a bite of the stew.

The flavor of the food exploded across all of her senses like a thunderstorm.

She'd never had anything in her life that was the equal to it. In the city all the food was prepackaged and uniform in taste which meant most of the time that it was rather tasteless.

Brett had often surmised that there were added in toxins, stimulants and hormones laced into the food because the pleasure girls were fed an entirely different diet. As much as had been possible she had switched her rations for theirs, while throwing her own away surreptitiously.

What she was eating now was actual to goodness real food!

She could actually sense the health in it as she ingested it down quickly.

The food was entirely too soon gone and mournfully she stared at the empty bowl.

Would she ever have food like this again?

Among the many simpler things she was lacking in proficiency with was the ability to simply cook. He could though.

If she stayed here he could teach her and she could eat like this all the time.

Pressing a hand to her head she shut down all thought or at least tried to.

What had this man done to her?

She didn't know, but her plans of resting went out the door.

She had to get out and away from this place right now!

Going to the door she turned the handle. It opened easily under the grip of her hand.

He hadn't even bothered to lock it.

In truth he probably hadn't wanted her to break out one of the skylight windows that lit up the whole interior of the house.

Stepping outside she took in the large clearing within the forest with wonder. Several acres of cleared forest lay all about her.

Half of it was left to be a rich verdant looking pasture of tall grass that made her ache to walk barefoot within it. The other half was divided up between vining trellises, small fruit trees, and extensive vegetable gardening.

The man was growing enough food here to feed an army!

Stepping out into the quaint beauty of a well tended place she advanced until at last she stood at the edge of where all civilization ended. It was actually hard to contemplate leaving such an idyllic setting for the unknown dangers of the forest beyond.

No matter - gathering her courage she turned away from the neatly ordered, but quaintly disarrayed homestead until it was at her back. The forest was before her with all of its dark brooding character rushing to the forefront.

In a word it came across as not only inherently dangerous, but also creepy. Closing her eyes she breathed out against the tension that she was feeling from within at leaving this place of plenty.

She could do it.

Yes, she was woman!

Her eyes opened and in stark horror she screamed as she fell over backwards and away from the creepily smiling visage of a creature that featured more teeth than anything else arrayed on its head.

Scrambling backward across the ground she waited for the raptor to pounce upon her and rip her to shreds.

It opened its mouth and hissed and Brett stopped moving even as her whole body quivered in the dread of what was about to happen. Then stooping forward the creature drug a giant curved claw through the dirt where the forest met the grass of the homestead enclosure.

Incredulously amazed at the display of intelligence involved in that action Brett looked up from the drawn line to the creature's face only to see it snap its mouth at her in a clear statement of what would happen if she took another step forward into the forest past the line carved into the dirt.

Brett needed no further convincing than that and gaining her feet she ran all the way back across the open land to the house that had been carved out of a mossy rock ledge upthrusting its way through the loamy dirt of the forest.

Reaching the door she cranked on the handle and as it opened she looked back furtively over her shoulder.

The raptor had not followed her into the clearing. It remained at the forest edge and then she watched in horror as two more stepped out of concealment that she hadn't even seen before this moment.

They seemed to communicate with each other and then abruptly all three scattered off in different directions and disappeared within seconds, but Brett knew better than to think that they'd gone very far.

Stepping inside she closed the door and as it clicked shut she sat down with her back to it.

Not being able to muster any control in the moment she let the big sobs that began to rise up from deep within her shake her even as she pressed her face against her drawn up knees.

She let her emotions have full reign over her and the predicament that she found herself ensnared within.

Eventually out of sheer weariness she sank over onto her side and as her tears wet the stone floor of the house her mind escaped into unconsciousness.

CHAPTER SEVEN

Curse Him!

The sweet sounds of birds chirping busily awakened Brett.

In panicked alarm she sat up.

Stiffly she tilted her head back and blinking she glanced at the brightness of the sun streaming down through the skylights up above.

It was too bright to be afternoon. Which meant that she'd slept through a whole day and a night!

She'd never slept so long in her life. Standing up and stretching she commented to herself on the reality that she also had never felt quite as refreshed as she did just now either.

Feeling thirsty she went to where a trickle of water fell in a constant rain from one corner of the cave room. She knelt beside the pool of water and tipping her hands into it she brought them up and drank.

The purity of the water she tasted was like drinking pure life into her being. Thirstier than ever for the essence of something so pure she continued to drink almost to the point of where she risked upsetting her stomach.

First it had been the food and now this. She had never realized something as simple as water could be so much better than anything she'd had before.

Getting up she ignored her resurgent hunger and went to the door. Pausing she reached over and picked up the chalk and drew a line on the wall next to the existing one.

She set the chalk piece down and cautiously opened the door.

All seemed to be blissfully peaceful outside. It was a lie though.

Brett watched the forest edge intently. She'd almost given up watching when suddenly a rock twitched slightly.

Abruptly, Brett slammed the door closed.

No way on earth was she going to set foot into that forest!

He'd been so right!

Curse him!

She couldn't let him be right!

With resurgent passion she opened the door and strode out into the sunlight.

So, if the forest was off-limits to her then what were her other options?

Turning her back to the forest she began climbing up onto the rocky upthrust that the cave house was carved out of.

Breathing heavy from the climb she reached the ceiling layer that lay over the cave below.

Bypassing the skylight windows she headed for the far side of what she could see was already an edge of some kind. It was the edge of a cliff.

Breathing shallow she cautiously approached the edge and looked over. Abruptly she moved back.

A chasm several hundred feet seemingly straight down had welcomed her gaze. She had not expected this at all.

Looking out over the vast panorama of forest that folded down from her sharply into the bottom of a valley she debated her options.

She was strong. She was a woman.

She did not need or want a man. So she would climb.

Yes, she would climb down. And there was no time like the present to get started less she stay and let her resolve weaken.

Now, she was going to show the high and mighty Mr. Ranvold what a woman was capable of.

With cautious trepidation she started down through a jagged jumble of boulders off to her left that offered her plentiful handholds for the moment.

Things went well for about an hour. She'd come down about 100 feet or so in elevation, but the easy handholds had disappeared.

Things were much more sheer now and Brett increasingly realized that this had been yet another mistake on her part.

Whether it was a man or a woman to attempt what she now was in the process of was simply just stupid.

She knew that now. Within the space of another white knuckled intense hour of scaling down the near vertical cliff face she inwardly confessed that all her pride was completely gone.

Breathing heavy she pressed her sweaty cheek to the stone that she clung against for dear life. She would go back...... if she could.

Just then her foot slipped and with a scream she fell as her fingers lost their grip. Her scream was cut short as she hit hard onto something that took all consciousness from her.

~~~~~~~~~

A sudden loud sound startled her. Blinking she opened her eyes.

It was raining and she was cold. It was also dark and stiffly Brett reached about and felt at her surroundings only to then see her predicament as a flash of lightning lit up the night as brightly as day for a moment.

She screamed in fright and huddled back against the cliff face as jagged lightning bolts continued to pound and dance all around her.

The rain continued to pour down and as it dribbled down her face she watched a tree on the opposite ridge get lit up into a ball of blue flame as it received a direct strike from a lightning bolt.

Brett quivered deeply in a way that had nothing to do with how cold she was. Nothing of this raw display of nature at play could be termed as something accidental.

There was a God, there simply had to be and the worst part of it was she knew in that moment that she didn't know Him and she was very much about to die.
~~~~~~~~~

Crying hysterically as the lightning blew a section of the rock away from the cliff not far from where she was she begged out loud, "Please!!! Oh please don't kill me!"

She fell onto her knees in the narrow area provided and begged over and over to a Divine entity that she'd never given the time of day to before in terms of existence, even as in fact it had been illegal for her to have done so. Now was different though.

Everything she had ever known was over and now more than ever she very much felt at the mercy of a higher power, whose presence she seemed to sense in the storm all around her.

Softly she begged, "If You let me live and I know I don't deserve to because...... because, I'm red with the blood of many. I killed them without mercy....but if You let me live though, I will try to do better. I will! I promise it!"

The veracity of the storm diminished suddenly and the pounding pressure of the rain eased to a gentle dribble and lifting her head Brett saw the first rays of dawn begin to creep over the horizon in the distance. Minutes stretched by and in dazzled wonder at the sheer beauty of it all she sat a spectator to a sunrise as if she had never seen one before.

As the sun came up higher into the sky her eyes drifted to the left as if they had been drawn to do so. Before the storm there had been literally no way off of the lonely perch that she had crashed down upon, but now because of the close by lightning strike and the resultant dislocation of rock she saw a clear way of escape.

The only thing though was that the way forward led upward and not downward.

Looking around not knowing where this mysterious force behind all creation might be she whispered, "Thank you."

With intense reflection she took in the full reality that the lightning strike had come before she had even begged for her life to be spared. A warm breeze seemed to kiss her cheek and shaking she touched her cheek because it seemed as if she'd been touched somehow.

"Return." Came a voice that seemed to be more inside her mind than something she'd heard with her ears and yet she found herself looking all around for a physical presence.

The voice was masculine sounding in its quality of force and yet elusive too in terms of a full understanding of it.

God was male?

If so, then no wonder that it had always been deemed illegal to dwell upon thoughts of what she now knew to be the case.

Shaking inwardly she moved to the task of climbing back up.

It was the first time in her life that she had ever submitted to the will of a masculine directive and with an inner quiver she knew it would not be the last time either. It took her all morning to get back up on top to the place where she'd started the day before, but in the end she made it.

In weak relief she slipped down the other side of the stone promontory and into the cabin. Quickly, she stripped her wet and ripped up clothes off until she was standing naked.

Grabbing up a blanket she shook as she cuddled into the warmth that it offered her. It smelled like him.

Why did he have to smell so good?

Longingly her eyes took in the lone bed situated in the room. Giving in she collapsed down upon it.

Her head hit the pillow and more of his scent rose up to fall about her. Even his scent was dominating her.

For the moment though there was simply nothing she could do about it and so she slept only to awaken in the late afternoon.

She made her first attempt at cooking only to soon find out that she was a complete failure at it.

She ate the food anyway. Later she went outside and stepped into the extensive garden that the man tended with what seemed almost loving regard.

With curiosity she took in the vast array of different growing species of plant material.

As her eyes gazed about she recognized the presence of what had to be weeds because they were apart from the established order that she saw everywhere else within the garden.

Kneeling down she pulled one weed up. It came out of the black dirt easily.

The next weed she encountered fought her efforts a bit more, but it gave way in the end as well.

Looking down at her dirt stained hands she wondered at herself as she'd never done anything like this before in her life. She liked it though.

She continued to work in the garden until the approaching night drove her to go back inside. Closing the door she stared at the marks on the wall for a long moment.

Taking the piece of chalk she drew another line. She put the chalk back in its place.

Like it or not she was going to be here when he got back.

CHAPTER EIGHT

To Kill or Not To Kill

Three Weeks Later

I stumbled slightly. Shaking my head I shook awareness back into focus and gratefully missed the tree that I'd been about to walk straight into.

In the gloom of twilight I recognized my surroundings. Finally, I was home.

With a birdlike twill Mandy came zipping up to me. I stroked a hand down her neck affectionately before saying, "Please tell me you didn't eat her."

She gave a negative head shake and patting her head I left the forest and stepped out onto the grass of my homestead.

The grass was getting a bit tall. I needed to cut it.

So much would need to be done. The garden was probably a complete.......blinking, I stared fixatedly in the semi darkness upon the ordered rows of my garden trying to discern if I was seeing things in my delirium or whether in fact my garden was indeed weed free.

Reaching down I felt at the dirt. It was indeed clear of all weeds.

I looked off to the house and saw light escaping from beneath the door. A palpable sense of relief shot through me then. She was still here.

Going to the door I opened it and stepped into the house. Immediately I noticed that things were different.

Not much, but some things were definitely in different places now.

I liked it. Different was good.

Slowly, my eyes traced from the familiar surroundings of my home to see her standing in the kitchen with that frightened deer look in her eyes. I didn't know what to say, only that I suddenly wished very much that she wasn't so afraid of me.

She was wearing one of my shirts that came down to lay about her thighs like a dress. She had it cinched into her narrow waist with a colorful piece of cloth.

I'd never seen a more beautiful and welcoming form of attire on a woman in my life. Despite my wounded condition I felt myself get achingly erect.

She was so beautiful that she practically left me tongue-tied. In fact she had left me tongue-tied.

"You're late." She whispered into the stillness.

I nodded and then taking my bloody hand away from my side I pointed to the outside and asked, "You weeded the garden?"

Reaching her hand up towards her face she did something absolutely beautiful then by simply folding some of the loose strands of hair back over one ear as she nervously said, "Yes, I hope that wasn't wrong of me."

"Good grief no! Thank you!"

Then before I knew it I was falling to the floor. I caught myself from making a complete idiot of myself by grabbing at a table nearby.

Suddenly a pair of strong little hands were also helping me complete the journey back up onto my feet. Quickly I moved forward across the space and sat down on my bed even as I mumbled out, "Thank you."

In utter exhaustion I looked longingly at the pillow with desire, but shaking my head to clear myself of that desire I lifted my shirt up instead. The wound had reopened and was bleeding freely.

Lethargically I started to get up, but a hand at my shoulder stopped the movement. Before my eyes then I watched as the old bandage was cut away from my side and I was treated to a new one being put in its place.

One much better done than my improvised one. I highly approved of the work.

I approved even more of the touch of her hands upon me and the sheer glory of her scent so close to me was electrifying.

Trying to focus I lifted a finger and with concern I touched the healing, but nasty looking scrape on the side of her forehead, "What happened?"

"I fell." She mumbled out as she finished her work.

The bandage done she started to move away, but I grasped her wrist.

Her eyes met mine as I with incredulous wonder asked, "You actually tried to climb down the cliff!"

She nodded.

"I have to say that I am impressed."

Looking down I took in the bandage held in place by a cloth wrapped around the muscular plain of my stomach and back. Never had I expected this of her upon my return.

It was well within her power in this moment to end my life.

Meeting her turbulent gaze I softly asked, "Am I going to wake up in the morning?"

Her face twisted with emotion and it came into her voice then as she said, "I haven't decided yet."

Nodding solemnly I said, "Well, in that case I better kiss you now or I might not get the chance to later."

Pulling her into me I brought my lips to rest down fully upon her cool ones and wetly I discovered them to be full and richly soft, even as I warmed them with mine for a long moment that could never have been long enough.

Reluctantly I let the source of raw energy that she was go and she pulled back quickly from me looking visibly rattled and breathing hard.

Gazing up at her I said, "Thank you, Olivia."

I lay down then and watching her I saw a tear of frustration slip down her cheek.

"My name is…."

"Olivia." I said interrupting and then my eyes were closed and I was lost to the world of the present, but hopefully not to the land of the yet living.

~~~~~~~~~

Brett pulled back further from the sleeping man. Her hand rose to her lips as if touching a foreign object.

She'd been kissed before by women, but never had it felt like that. Never had it felt so right.

Turning quickly she went back to the kitchen and gripped the edge of the table hard as her eyes stared down upon the knife that lay there. It would be so easy.

All her torment would be over. All she had to do was slice his throat as he slept.

Picking the knife up she threw it viciously.

It sailed through the air to thud heavily into the door of the cave house.

It stuck their fixed into the door just as it should have been in him earlier when he'd come in through it. She'd been standing ready, as she had every day for a week and yet in the moment she'd froze.

Now he was at her complete mercy and she was doing nothing!

What was wrong with her?!

In frustration she sat down in one of the chairs. He began to snore slightly and along with the crackle of the fire it was the only noise in the room.

Far from being annoying the sound of his snoring was actually somewhat comforting because now she wasn't alone. She picked up the one book that had been banned more than all others by her society.
~~~~~~~~~

It was a book that she'd been reading from now most nights. Among many things witnessed within its pages was the reality of a world wherein men and women lived with each other.

A world in which women openly submitted to the male that had been given headship over them by God Himself. It was hard to stomach and yet there seemed to be an order to it.

She started to read again, but her mind simply wasn't in it.

Her hand rose to her lips and felt at them again.

She glanced toward the bed. It was almost like he'd put a seal of some kind upon her with his touch.

Already she felt possessed by him and nothing of him had even entered into her, not even his tongue.

Why did the remembered feeling of his lips upon hers make her stomach twitch and flutter as if it was full of butterflies?

Why was she damp between her thighs?

Why did she insanely yearn even in this moment to still be in the act of being kissed by him?

She closed the Bible that lay upon her lap and held it against her chest as she contemplated the oddities enfolding in her that were a reversal to the reality that she had always known. Tiredly as her mind whirled with both objections and positives to the things she debated upon the simple need for sleep became overwhelming.

The only problem was that he had the comfy bed. It wasn't a very big bed, and as it was if she was to ever lay with him she would have to half lay on him to fit.

Abruptly along with that thought and all that it entailed her inner thighs went from being damp to entirely soaked. So much so that she could literally smell her arousal in the air.

There was no denying the reality that despite the objections raised in her mind and spirit her body clearly wanted to be dominated and very much taken possession of.

She'd heard the whispered stories told by older women to the pleasure girls of how it had once been like.

The female lovers that she'd been forced to have in order to be deemed normal had sometimes used dildos on her, but they had never been all that satisfying. It was going to be very different with him.

Tears streaked down her face.

It was really going to happen.

Crying softly she remained in the chair and left the knife stuck in the door knowing that she'd regret it in the morning, but in the moment she was powerless to stop the inevitable.

CHAPTER NINE

A New Day

It was early, but the lamp was still burning enough to see by. Idly, I let my hand close over the handle of the knife stuck firmly in the door and with effort I managed to tug it free.

What a wildcat she was.

Walking softly across the room not wanting to startle her I laid the knife down on the arm of the chair she was sleeping all curled up in.

She looked cold and so I covered her with a blanket.

Going outside I got what I needed and coming back in I set about the process of making breakfast. Her head popped up at the sounds that I was making in the kitchen.

I saw her briefly hesitate over the knife, but rising up she left it on the arm of the chair as blanket around her she came closer to view what I was doing.

Curious as to her attention I remained silent as she aptly regarded everything I was doing with great interest.

Finally the breakfast preparation was ready for baking. I set the acorn flour dough covered casserole into the metal sides of what had once been called a Dutch Oven a very long time ago.

"How did you learn to do all that?" She asked softly.

I shrugged, "Some of it by experimentation, some from what I remember of my mother's cooking, and yes, I did have a mother."

I watched a small smile tug at the corners of her mouth but then she turned away.

Something came to mind then suddenly and with a bit of worry I asked, "What about you, your mother I mean, was she still……"

Olivia shook her head '*no*', and then said, "In the city we were never allowed to know our mothers. The breeding women were kept separate and regardless of that fact I know that she's dead as two years ago they killed all the stud slaves and right along with them the breeding women because of possible tainting."

I waited for her to look up and when she did at long last I said, "I'm sorry."

She shrugged as if it was no big deal. It was a very big deal.

Time went by with neither of us talking then.

Finally she spoke, "The cities?"

"All gone."

She nodded.

Hugging her arms about herself I saw her struggle against speaking for several moments before finally relinquishing by saying, "I…… I think….. I think that was the right thing to do. What you did I mean along with the others like you that is, in relation to the cities I mean."

"It does me well to hear you feel that way Olivia. For myself I am only too grateful for the time that is ahead of us with all the possibilities that might be brought forth by not being hunted all the time. Already the men are talking about moving out of the forest with their families, but as for myself I actually like it here. I think I'll stay. Yes." I said nodding my head even as the imagery of flat open countryside really held no appeal to me.

Somehow such a landscape was simply just too easy to survive in.

Her voice sounding very low I heard her murmur, "Why do you call me Olivia?"

She'd asked the question but she was looking away from me as if she didn't want to actually hear an answer.

Picking my words carefully I said, "The name has always been beautiful sounding to me. You are beautiful. What, in my own opinion, I have done is to rescue you from a lifestyle as well as the role you played in a past life into a new way of life and hence I think the journey is worthy of a new name and Olivia is the name that comes to mind when I look at you."

She said nothing, but remained quiet and very thoughtful looking.

"Olivia?"

Her head lifted and her troubled eyes met mine.

"Ready for breakfast?"

"Yes."

In that moment it was hard not to shout out and pound my chest like some kind of primal beast, because in that one-word answer I knew I had succeeded. She would be mine.

She would submit, but dutifully I tamped all my elation down out of respect for the effort I knew becoming as she was now had cost her.

Pulling back a chair at the table I waited for her to come to it.

Slowly, she came and sat down and I eased her into the table even as I knew soon that I would be easing my aching cock into her willing body. Leaning down I kissed possessively down onto the exposed side of her neck.

Her breathing hitched sharply, but she did nothing to move away even as I tasted her skin with my tongue. I stayed only a moment and pulling back I stepped completely away.

My erection was now such that I could've broken down the door with it. I had not expected her to be half as sweet as she was turning out to be.

Passionate, yes, but sweet, I hadn't seen that one coming.

Her sweetness bore developing so that in time it would be what ruled her passion. To that end I could wait for her final submission.

I would wait.

Pulling the casserole out of the oven I fixed up two plates and then moving to the table I set one down before her and the other at my place across from her. I saw her burn her mouth on a bite, but stubborn lass that she was she kept shoveling the hot food into her already scalded mouth.

In truth I felt like groaning as I watched her mouth move. She glanced at me and abruptly stilled.

"What?"

"It's time to pray."

I asked the blessing over the food and then I went about feeding my own raging appetite all the while denying the inner beast that wanted to feast on the beauty seated across from me. Looking away from her and down at my remaining food I fought hard to chain away the beastly passions that just looking at her inspired.

It was useless. I knew what I wanted.

So what though. Some things simply had to be done a certain way and my penis was not going to do my thinking for me.

Looking up at her I asked, "Would you like to accompany me on a walk after breakfast?"

Her head popped up immediately, "Where?"

"Into the forest."

"I...... I..."

"I'll keep you safe. I promise. Well, do you want to accompany me or not?"

She nodded.

"Good, finish up then and we'll be on our way."

CHAPTER TEN

"What's wrong?"

The forest about us was still, the silence broken only by the sound of a solitary songbird high up in the branches here and there. I'd taken no weapons as there was simply no need to do so.

Olivia though looked unsteadily about, ahead and behind her in a repetitive fashion.

Smiling I said, "They're gone."

"How do you know?"

"Because I told them to go. They have families of their own to attend to."

"How did you do it? How did you get control of them, the monsters I mean?"

Nodding to her question I said, "One day I'll show you, I'll even teach you to talk to them yourself if you wish."

My hand reached out then and I claimed hers and in surprise she walked along with me allowing her hand to be joined with mine.

She made no effort to pull hers free of mine. That was a good thing, as I had no intention of letting it go.

The path we were going down was getting increasingly damp in nature and as we continued on a growing roar could be heard in the distance.

I saw genuine interest lighting up Olivia's face as she waited to see what she no doubt by now had deduced would be a waterfall.

Rounding a bend in the trail we came out onto a promontory point and there before us was the visual evidence of thousands upon thousands of gallons of water cascading over a sharp precipice only to pound down terrifically upon the jagged rocks far below. It was breathtaking to behold and the sight of it had stolen all of Olivia's attention.

I watched her with keen interest as she gazed at the water falling in the distance. She shivered suddenly as it was quite cool here and spying a nearby smooth barked tree I moved to lean back against it and when I did I pulled Olivia to be directly in front of me.

Folding my arms possessively around her I brought her back to rest against the blazing warmth of my body that wished to do nothing more than possess hers even as the desire to heat her up from within with my cock was as much of a raging torrent as the display of water before us was.

I wasn't going back on my word though.

She would break before I did. Once upon a time I had broken Maria.

I had done it the hard way. In some ways I was ashamed of myself looking back now upon our first times together.

In truth I'd raped her without remorse at the time. Things were different now though.

I didn't want to be that man anymore. That said, I wanted the woman pressed up against me in pursuit of warmth every bit as much as I had wanted Maria.

The only difference this time was me. I was different.

There had to be a better way to have what I wanted. So help me though I simply couldn't resist the girl in my arms.

Slowly, I let my head lower until my lips warmly kissed soundly down upon the side of her neck. She jerked and tried to move forward, but my arms held her put.

She could've certainly put up a bigger fight, but she didn't and I took that for the invitation it was and slowly began to relish the body of my woman for the first time.

My hands moved upon her. Always holding her, but stroking all that she was and as my lips pressed kisses out against her neck and shoulder I didn't miss the feel of her body push in against my hands slightly or how she came up on her tip toes as both of my hands came up her flanks to fill themselves with the glorious weight of her breasts.

She moaned.

With that uttered sound of pleasure from off her lips I turned her in my arms and met her troubled eyes that stared into mine in a search for answers.

The only answer I gave her was to kiss her. I kissed her hard with all the passion that I had for her.

She didn't fight other than to struggle to remain standing as I bent her over backward with the force of my kiss.

She needn't have bothered to support herself.

Turning I pressed her up against the tree even as I plunged my tongue into her mouth and tasted all that her sweet mouth had to offer me. My hands held, squeezed, and molded all that they could reach of her.

Nothing of her was off-limits to them. Pulling back from her face briefly I heard her gasp for air and I watched as her eyes opened with a clear sense of shock to be seen in them.

She liked it. I could see it.

She turned her head to the side then as if to say that she had not surrendered when in truth I knew that was not so. My fingers undid the colorful sash cinching my shirt in to her narrow waist.

Her eyes came back to me and I read within them an acceptance of what was happening along with a fear of the unknown. It still wasn't what I was looking for though.

Taking a free hanging wrist I bound it loosely with the sash to her other one.

Breathing heavy she asked, "Why are you tying me up? I....I haven't fought you, have I?"

Letting go of her bound together hands both of mine swept up to encapsulate her beautiful face as I said, "You haven't willingly submitted either. Now if you really wanted to you could pull your hands-free couldn't you?"

The reality of my words was clearly evident.

Taking her loosely bound hands I lifted them. "Think of this as a way to let go and simply enjoy what I'm about to do to you."

She shivered in my grasp and with a husky sounding voice she asked, "What are you going to do to me?"

Smiling, I said, "You'll see."

Taking the leftover end of the sash I hooked it over a branch above her head and raising her hands I tied them off above her head. She could've easily pulled them free, but she didn't even as once more I began to kiss her.

I simply loved the taste of her mouth, but I wanted the true taste of her even more. Working my way down I kissed through the material of my shirt upon what lay beneath as she stood offered for the taking by her own choice of will.

Her hands stayed tied above her head even as I undid the laces of her boots and pulled them both off of her feet. My hands slid beneath the hem of my shirt that fell about her like a dress.

Her pants came undone and I stripped them down along with her panties and lifting each of her legs I pulled the pants free only to then sideways toss them into the rapids below.

"What! Why?" She exclaimed with protest, only to stop as my hands drug the material of my shirt upward.

I uncovered the beautiful apex of her thighs and then her hips and holding the shirt up I wetly kissed and dug my tongue into the cleft of her warm belly button.

I tied a knot in my shirt so it wouldn't fall back down and then both hands grasping a hold of her naked hips I looked up and said, "There will be no pants in your attire from now on, only skirts and dresses. Got it."

She stared at me with desire even as she tried not to express the reality of the trepidation of the moment that she was experiencing.

Slowly, she nodded her head then.

As a reward my mouth fell to kiss softly upon her waist and she jerked even as bit by bit I felt her breathing pick up as I licked and kissed my way across the beautiful terrain that she had to offer me. I brought her forward away from the tree as my mouth found her even as I lifted one of her luscious thighs to slide over one of my shoulders.

She cried out as she hung from her wrists even as my tongue drank in how incredibly wet she was for me.

Panting she pressed against my lips and tongue and when she came it was a thing of utter beauty.

I saw a squeal of raw pleasure peel off from her lips that looked as if they were doing everything they could to stifle it. As I licked, suckled and softly bit her tenderly through the duration of her orgasm a series of ever mounting moans began escaping from her.

I brought her under orgasm again and again with just the use of my mouth upon her wet sex. Her heady moans became a scream and then she bucked against my open mouth as I devoured her through the heat of another orgasm that had more intensity to it than all the ones before it.

Suddenly her hands were free and gripped about on my head but not in a concerted effort to dislodge it. She held me to her and almost with the intensity of one giving childbirth she's screamed in a completely uninhibited fashion as yet another orgasm more complex and complete than the prior several ripped through her body.

Her screams were drowned out only partially by the roar of the waterfall in the background. I heard each of them with relish even as I felt her body trembling with the passion I had provoked.

I let go of the wet clamped down pressure that I had been putting upon her clitoris and eased her thigh from off my shoulder.

She stood there shaking badly as she leaned back against the tree for support. Her eyes were crammed shut as if afraid to open them and see the reality that this moment was real.

Smiling I bent forward and folded her over my shoulder.

She gasped at my unexpected action but gave no resistance as I began to walk down the path towards the roar of water.

Her beautiful rear was right beside my face and it was beyond hard to remain focused. All I wanted was her, but she wasn't mine until she gave me everything and she was the only one who could do so and even as that was how I had limited myself the games would just have to continue.

After ten minutes of descent down the trail and with the waterfall sounding more muted in the background I set her back down on her feet again. She backed up slightly and tugged at the knot in her shirt dress that continued to allow her to be bare to my eyes from the waist down.

"Olivia."

She stopped tugging at the knot and then slowly glanced up to my eyes.

"Take it off." I spoke with authority and yet in truth I had no idea what she would do.

Slowly, her hands lifted and then my shirt was being dropped onto the ground even as she stood almost completely bare before me. My eyes took in the stretchy material that passed for a bra that bound her breasts away from my view.

My her eyes rose from her breasts to meet hers and speaking I said, "Just like the pants."

She glanced at the raging river behind her and shivered. Nothing happened.

She wasn't obeying. Still, I stayed calm.

Then biting her lip I saw her hands slowly lift up. The bra came undone and with reluctance it slipped from her fingers into the raging current nearby.

She stood naked highlighted by the sun and slowly I took my own clothes off until I was as she was save for my bandage. Her gaze settled down upon my cock and then danced away.

Amusingly I watched it come back only to move away again. Again the action was repeated.

It was almost comical to behold, only I knew it wasn't something funny at all for her.

"Olivia?"

Her eyes rose to mine.

"What's wrong?"

Her hand lifted to nervously brush at her hair and I admired with desire the swing of her breasts the size of full apples that was brought about by the action.

Her breasts weren't overly large, but they were full and her nipples were engorged to the max as if in temptation to be bitten and suckled upon.

Whispering she said, "It will never fit! I....I...."

I stepped closer and she looked about as if for evaluation of whether to run or not, but hesitatingly she remained in place as if she had no other good option to choose from. The wet tip of my engorged cock pressed into the soft pool of her belly and she looked away from it and then back again.

I lifted her head with a finger under her chin and gazing warmly into her eyes I soothed, "It will fit."

"It's huge! Everything about you... I... why me?"

"I told you. I want you."

"I....I....I'm scared."

"You think I'll hurt you?"

She looked down. Then she shook her head '*no*'.

Reaching my hands up I squeezed down reassuringly over her bare shoulders.

Her eyes lifted and softly I coaxed, "What is it Olivia? Tell me."

"I....I've never felt like this. I... I actually want......"

She looked away, but I brought her face back with a finger and she burst out with, "I want you in me and I don't even know why! All my life I was taught that men were bad. Always about how just...... completely bad....and....and....you are bad....but you're not...... you're going to dominate me and I hate that and...... and yet some part of me loves that you will...... I don't know....I..."

"Shhh." I said and wrapping my arms around her I pulled her in for a full body hug up against me.

Shaking in my grasp I felt her arms come around me tentatively and the firmness of my hug upon her gradually became reciprocated by her, even as her breathing softened.

Whispering into her hair I said, "Could you maybe lift or lower that right arm of yours an inch or two."

She gasped abruptly and whispered, "Sorry." as she moved her arm away from the bandage on my side.

Her hand fell to my hip and it stayed there as she continued to breathe in deeply with her nose pressed up against my chest.

Speaking I said, "You were raised in a very unnatural setting and for that matter so was I. For the first time in really both of our lives we're about to experience something entirely natural. It's natural for you to want me even as it's natural for me to want you. Forget the past and try to live right here in this moment."

I let go of her. Her gaze remained downcast even as the stiff broadness of my shaft remained in contact with her belly that it had drizzled pre-cum all across.

Speaking in a low voice she said, "You said before you left that I would submit to you in the most vulnerable of ways a woman can submit to a man. What did you mean by that?"

She looked up into my eyes and I gave it to her straight.

"The first time my cock will come into your body it won't be in through your vagina, but rather it will be in through your beautiful ass. The reason for this is that when the day comes you can offer me that vulnerable part of you to me then I will know that I have all of you and I want nothing less than your full and complete surrender of literally all of you to me."

She broke contact with me and backing up she exclaimed loudly, "You're crazy!"

"Maybe I am. Once more I will have you to know that I don't intend to torment myself for weeks or months on end. If what I've said is beyond you then you're free to go. I won't lift a finger to stop you."

She stared at me in a complete daze even as her lips whispered, "You're serious aren't you. You'd actually let me go."

I nodded.

She turned sideways and looked away towards the downstream current.

Shaking her head her gaze came to land on mine and then back upon the river.

She was crying.

Her arms rose to hug over her breasts and I saw her shiver despite the warmth of the sun.

I broke my stance and coming up behind her I stepped in close and pulled her against me with my arms. The wet head of my shaft glided up the top part of the cleft of her bottom to rest against her indented spine even as the thickest part of my erection now warmly split apart the cheeks of her heart shaped rear with its mass.

She shivered but made no effort to be free. Then to my surprise she began shaking her head '*yes*' even as tears dropped down to land upon my arms that were crossed over top of hers.

My erection swelled even larger and she felt the change instantly even as she expressed her fears outwardly with, "Oh God!"

Her body jerked as the emotion of her tears made effect upon it and I heard her choke out over the sobs, "I don't want to leave. I....I like the house. I like your garden. I like how different everything is from all that I've ever known. I liked the pleasure that you gave me on the way here. I..... I even like how good you can cook. I like that a lot actually. And I also like that you seem to be a man of integrity. I don't like a lot of things about you though. And yet the reality is that I have nowhere to go even if I were to leave. I have no family! I have no one and....and I don't even know how to cook!"

She shook in my arms with the emotion of all she was expressing. Not being able to take it any longer I turned her and as I did her arms came about me tightly.

I said nothing but continued to simply hold her to me. Long moments passed by and finally she pushed back and when she did I let her go.

My hands fell to her hips and I waited for her to speak as she stared at my erection that rose up between us, still proudly full of the passion I had to have her.

Slowly her gaze rose to mine and wetting her lips she said, "I've never had anything in my ass. I saw other girls do things, but I....I never. I understand that this is a test on your part of me and I actually respect that, but....I want to stay. So...... yes. My answer is yes. I will submit to you. I will do whatever you want, but please I....I...." Her head lowered with the rest unsaid.

"Please what, Olivia?" I pressed.

"Can you seriously not see that that is not going to fit." She whispered out without looking up at me.

In response to that I chuckled and said, "Yes, Olivia it will. Maria was a smaller statured girl than you and yet it fit all the way in wherever I chose to put it."

Her head came up and I watched her read the truth in my gaze.

"Did it hurt her?"

"Not the way I did it."

Her eyes searched mine a moment longer and then with a shaky breath she whispered, "I suppose you want to do it now."

"Hell no!"

Her eyes blinked with surprise, "What?"

"I just want you to submit to me Olivia. I'll take your ass, your vagina, your mouth, everything, but I'm no longer a beast that would press something upon you in a way that would hurt you. Once upon a time I would have, but I'm not that man anymore."

She blinked repetitively several times, before whispering, "You're going to try to not make it hurt?"

"Yes."

Her arms crossed over her breasts then even as with a stronger voice then she asked, "Why did you make me think you were going to… going to… you know what!"

"I didn't. You merely assumed the worst case scenario."

She stared at me for a long moment and then glanced to the ground before softly admitting, "You're right, I did."

It was a day full of victories.

"I have a request of you, Olivia."

She glanced up with interest.

"I want, no-o, make that I need – an orgasmic release."

She glanced down at my erection and then quickly up at me.

Shyly she brushed at a wayward strand of hair near her face and with her action of uncovering her breasts I could see that she was willing.

Reaching a hand out I pressed it down upon her shoulder and she quickly got the hint. Gracefully she knelt down and my eyes left her to stare down river as I felt her mouth open over the head of my shaft and close warmly about it as she welcomed it into the hot wet cave of her mouth.

I groaned and within seconds it seemed I was spewing my seed deeply into the depths of her mouth. I heard her half choke, but her lips stayed put stretched about my shaft even as I felt her throat swallow repeatedly.

Opening my eyes I looked down upon her head as she pulled her lips free of my shaft. Reaching a finger up she wiped at a stream of semen that had escaped her lips and had flowed down to drip off her chin.

I saw her stare at the milky substance for only a moment before she licked her finger clean.

"Why did you do that?"

She glanced up and with a slight shrug she said, "I knew you were watching."

"And that matters why?"

"I thought it would please you."

"Why would you want to please me?"

"Your letting me stay and….and you promised to please me. It seemed like the right thing to do, right? I mean, in your book it says to treat others as you would like to be treated. I…."

Lifting her up into my arms I said, "I couldn't be more pleased."

I walked away from the river and with trepidation she asked, "Where are we going?"

"Oh, right over here to these hot spring pools where I thought that I might work on pleasing you again like I just did up against the tree."

Her gaze went from me to take in the lifting clouds of steam nearby and I saw the corner of her mouth tilt upward in a smile.

"Would you like that, Olivia?"

"I would." She said before blushing beat red from her boldness to ask me to put my mouth back on to her sex.

I stepped into the warm water and as I did so I let her legs down until she had slipped waist deep into the warm water. As her flesh made contact with the warm water she let out with a groan of pleasure at the experience of the warm water upon her chilled flesh.

I sat down on a sunken boulder and pulled her in close to me.

"But first I'm going to make the acquaintance of these two beauties." I said in reference to her breasts that now bobbed before my face with ebullient splendor.

Shyly her one hand rose and pointing to her left breast she said, "This is Kylie and this one is Olga."

I stared at her breasts and then up into her eyes in complete shock for a moment.

Then I saw it.

She'd been pulling my leg!

A peel of laughter shook free from her and as it did she turned about in the water to try to escape, but she wasn't quick enough.

I caught her and hauled her back in and with aggression I bent her down until her lips were on mine.

I kissed her and had the pleasure of feeling her respond back in kind. Breaking off the kiss I pulled her in even closer as I held both of her wrists behind her back with one of my hands.

My lips left her to hotly claim over one of her engorged nipples and she gasped out loudly only to then deeply moan as a finger from my free hand came up to press between her thighs.

She jerked in my grasp, but my hold upon her wrists and her nipple were secure.

I watched her gaze captively down at me as I aggressively suckled her breast, even as she now had one of my fingers firmly seated all the way up inside of her.

Breathing heavy she gasped out, "I..... Oh, God...... I'm so glad...so glad, I said yes! Ohhhhhhhh!!!"

Smiling, I let her nipple and areola pop free from my lips only to claim her other one with an equal aggression as I had the first.

Which one of the beautiful twins it was at the moment I wasn't quite sure, but it was quickly learning that I was its new master.

She began to softly cry out my name as I provoked yet another orgasm to rise to the surface within her. She came hard and as she did so I let her wrists go.

Her knees weakly collapsed and she came down to rest against me.

Her head pressed sideways to my chest even as her hands held on loosely to my shoulders and yet her body continued to shake from the orgasm that seemed to be ongoing even as I felt the throb of her womanhood tightly compressed about my finger still buried to the hilt within her.

After a long moment she murmured out, "Can we stay here for a while?"

Speaking out against her hair I rumbled huskily "I don't have anywhere to be. Do you?"

Raising her head she smiled softly even as she said, "No, I don't."

She kissed me then and I let her have her way against my lips even as I relished the freedom that she was finding in her submission to me.

CHAPTER ELEVEN

Emotions in the Night

'Olivia.'

It was a nice name. It was now her name.

Shyly, Olivia lifted her head slightly.

Instantly the big hand spread across her entire hip squeezed possessively even as its owner remained fast asleep.

Olivia couldn't help the thrill that shook through her entire being at the simple touch of his broad hand gripping her flesh.

Inwardly she shook as the new delight of her situation swept throughout her being.

The unexpected delight of belonging to a man. Not just any man, but this man in particular.

The strength and hard feel of him up against her was like some forbidden nirvana that she couldn't believe that she had been kept away from for so long. Where once there had been fear of his far greater strength than hers now there was nothing but absolute peace.

This man could do anything with her that he wanted to, but the point that he had made very clear was that his intentional pursuit of her was rooted firmly in the reality that he wanted her to enjoy his complete and total possession of her. He did not want her fear, but rather he wanted her respect.

Olivia let her head rest back down upon the heavy muscled bicep beneath her ear even as her whole back was treated to the feel of his chest and ribbed abdomen pressing up against her. Her bottom lay nestled in against his groin held there by the hand at her hip.

She was not going to be allowed to escape. Indeed she no longer wanted to escape.

Laying still with eyes wide open in the darkness of the night Olivia quietly contemplated on the reality of her master's massive shaft that now lay peacefully at rest and feeling deceptively small up against her bottom. Tomorrow it would be once more hard and without a doubt she knew that she was going to feel every inch of his thick cock glide deeply into an area of her body that no one had ever even touched before.

Well, he had.

Olivia blushed and felt her thighs grow damp as she remembered the pool of hot mineral water from the prior morning.

After he had given her the first orgasms they had kissed and kissed and then things had gotten a lot more serious. She'd found herself spun about in the water and flipped over a smoothly warm boulder with her face but inches above the surface of the bubbling water before her.

She'd thought it had been the end. As the water had lapped about her thighs on the other side of the boulder she had felt the heat of his two big hands as they gripped the cheeks of her bottom and stretched them widely apart.

In that moment she'd thought it had been the moment of his promised possession of her and dutifully she had remained lying prone over the rock with the expectation of soon screaming in agony as his huge cock forced its way up into her tight ass.

That hadn't happened though. Instead as she'd lain there breathing hard with the expectation of the worst about to happen his hands had pushed her cheeks back closed only to then open them up again.

Again and again he'd done it even as his large hands had squeezed and powerfully kneaded the pliant flesh that he held.

Olivia had soon found herself moaning and clutching onto the rock with pleasure at the oddly unexpected pleasure of feeling her ass be worked about in his hands.

It was a far cry from the agony that she had been expecting. In a way his massaging touch of her bottom had relaxed her in a way that she'd never experienced before in life and then in the height of that brought on peace of massaging comfort he'd done something entirely unexpected.

Olivia's eyes closed tightly and reflexively she rubbed her bottom back against the cock she both feared and hungered for at the same moment as she remembered what had happened the prior morning.

In her mind's eye she fully remembered the feel of his warm lips against the entrance to her bottom. The touch of his lips there had been absolutely startling.

In fact it had been shockingly wonderful and then it had been made only more wonderful by the actions of his powerful tongue that had started to lick her there, even as one of his big fingers had pierced through the lips of her womanhood to deeply seat itself within the bounds of her femininity.

As his thick and very wet plunging finger owned the depths of her womanhood he had continued the assault of his lips and mouth against her bottom entrance to the point that his tongue had actually penetrated her there. The strange and yet wonderfully erotic sensations had simply been too much and in the here and now Olivia only remembered too well the euphoria with which she had gripped down onto the boulder and cried out with the pleasure that had been provoked out of her by her man's masterful touch upon her flesh.

Upon the culmination of her orgasm she'd started to lift up off the boulder only to feel his hand commandingly press her back down. At that moment she'd been ready.

Meekly she'd lain stretched over the boulder more than willing to accept his cock into her ass, even if it hurt as bad as she expected it to.

Instead she had got the wet finger that had been driving her womanhood crazy with need slowly pressed in against the entrance of her ass.

He hadn't pressed it in hard or in any way been aggressive, but instead with a gentle pressure he had penetrated it into her with little resistance all the way up into her until his knuckles were pressed against the cleft of her ass.

During the process of his finger's invasion of virgin territory Olivia had found herself exhaling deeply and pushing out against his invasion as if in welcome to whatever he wanted to do to her.

Within just a few short seconds she had been amazed at the reality of his big finger becoming seated all the way into her.

Where was the pain?

Staring wide-eyed at the water she'd instead surprised herself further by issuing out a moan of remorse as he pulled his finger clear of her ass. Thankfully the action had only been a short-lived one as he had brought it thickly back into her all over again.

She had moaned out loud again with the odd feel of experiencing something seemingly unnatural that instead in the moment felt entirely natural. It was hard to explain, but somehow she belonged to this man and it was only right for him to be exploring her as he now was.

The feeling of his finger firmly seated in an area of her anatomy that had been previously untouched was both very odd feeling and not without some discomfort, but there was something else to. She felt full.

The fullness felt good and then with his other hand he had pressed two of his fingers within her vagina to the hilt. She had never felt more full in her life in that moment and she'd come instantly screaming on the spot, only to orgasm again and again as the fingers within her vagina plunged with aggression as the finger in her ass slowly twisted back and forth only to withdraw a little to then be pressed fully back in again.

His possessing fingers entirely dominated her and Olivia had shook apart at the seams gripped by pleasures to extreme to even have imagined something like this was possible.

Now laying in the dark held in the steely clasp of a man that had given her so much pleasure and awoken an erotic need within her for even more it was hard to think about anything else than to wish that he was awake so that everything that had been done to her yesterday could be done again and again and again to her once more.

Biting her lip she lay there in his relaxed grip as she remembered how at last he had finally stopped. Crying she had come up off the rock as his fingers left her.

Turning about she had collapsed to her knees in the warm water and hugged the man who she now belonged to with a passion she could not fully comprehend. His shaft had been a burning tower of desire pressed up against her ear and looking up at him through crying eyes, even as the ache for more pleasure beckoned, she for the first time in her life had begged for something from a man.

She'd begged him to put his cock into her. He'd shaken his head no and with tightlipped control that she could only marvel at he'd said, "Tomorrow."

Even as his hands found her head and positioned it in place for his dribbling cock to press wetly through her swollen lips.

As if by instinct she had immediately suckled down upon his flesh and once more he exploded within her mouth bathing it with copious amounts of his hot seed.

She'd swallowed and swallowed but still some of it had dribbled from the corners of her lips even as it came pumping jet after jet into her. The man was a complete stud and hungrily she'd consumed the essence of him that in some way seemed to have already evoked a possession of her because of the way that she now hungered for it.

Wherever he wanted to put his seed was fine by her.

Olivia turned in the dark then knowing that she risked waking both her captor and possessor, but she couldn't help it.

The remembered taste of him was just simply too much.

Feeling emotional to the point of tears she broke his hold on her hip and eased down on the narrow bed until her face was nuzzled into the masculine aroma of his maleness.

Opening her mouth she captured the head of his shaft and felt it begin to pulse with life and rapid growth in size even as one of his hands rubbed at her head in a gesture that could only be described as affectionate.

How had he done this to her?

How had he remade her over into this creature of intense desire and want for everything that was male about him?

The answer remained elusive even as she accepted the reality that she now desired to be this man's plaything, his constant companion, the bearer of his children, and his faithful companion for the rest of his life.

He groaned deeply as she with wet slurpful action went about learning the process of giving him pleasure with the actions of her tongue and mouth. Minutes went by and inwardly she rejoiced as she heard his pleasure sound out even as she could feel it in the tremble of his hips and legs beneath her.

He cried out then and the jetting pulse of his seed into the warm cave of her mouth had her suddenly groaning herself.

Doing her best to breathe and focus she felt her inner core seize up and then crash apart in waves of pleasure.

Gasping about the hard shaft filling her mouth she experienced the orgasm that swept through her loins as if it had been manually provoked from her, while in truth she hadn't even been touched.

Crying emotionally she pulled her swollen lips up off his shaft even as some of his seed and her excess saliva dribbled from her lips to mix with her tears that were falling upon his abdomen.

In a word she was a complete mess and making a mess of him as well. She went to wipe at her face only to feel her whole form hauled up his and then it was his lips hotly pressed to hers that registered more than anything.

Embarrassed by both her emotion and the mess she tried to pull back, only he wouldn't let her. It was very clear that he didn't care about the mess or even tasting himself on her lips.

Indeed it seemed like the only thing he cared about was her. When the reality of that noteworthy concept made full impact with her conscious mind to dwell upon the kiss ended.

She let her gaze be shyly downcast in the darkness even as she felt a blush tinge across her cheeks, even as she remained straddled over his stomach in wonderment as to what he would do next.

Seeming to know in what a tender state of emotional condition she was in he was the first to move.

First he wiped her cheeks clear of tears and then her lips and then he was pulling her down against his side to be cuddled up against him. Olivia with a long release of tensioned air let herself relax as she slipped into the sublime feeling of what it was like to feel her soft feminine form pressed up against the rigidity of his masculine body.

~~~~~~~~~

Laying in the dark I watched as her eyes traced over the nakedness of my form that she lay cuddled up against. She seemed especially taken by the shadowy outline of my manhood which still stood achingly erect with the desire I had to plunge it into her.

Slowly, then I felt her hand drift from her side out across me until her fingers gently gripped about the base of my shaft.

Her voice sounding still somewhat gripped by emotion she asked, "In the morning will you please start to teach me how to cook like you do?"

The question at this moment in time was unexpected and something maybe that would've caused me to laugh at some other point, but I sensed that there was a lot more to her question then lay on the surface.

Entirely serious I replied, "It would be my pleasure."
~~~~~~~~~

Her gaze rose to mine in the semi darkness and coming in even closer against me she brought her hand that had been gripping my shaft up to lay over my heart. She said nothing and within moments I detected that she had fallen asleep utterly content to be where she was.

CHAPTER TWELVE

"Yes, Master."

Cooking was not going well. We had already burned several omelets, but with determination I continued to do my best to steer her in the direction needing to be gone.

Her clear lack of even being able to fix something for herself suitable to eat was astounding, but I didn't mention a word about it.

She hadn't said much, but then with a frustrated puff of air that ruffled the hair about her face she grabbed on to my wrist and shook it slightly.

I got the notion that she wanted me to let go of the skillet wherein I was trying to salvage the latest disaster of her making. I set the skillet to the side and let go and as I did she pulled my hand and then my other hand until both of them were palm up before her.

Leaning in she pressed a kiss that burned of a hidden fire into the palm of each of my hands and then stepping in close she brought my hands around her to rest on her bottom.

She released my wrists and placing hers over the top of my shoulders she leaned up on tiptoe even as my fingers reflexively gripped upon the cheeks of her bottom to aid her in the attainment of height she needed in order to wetly kiss me for a brief moment before saying, "I really suck at this."

Chuckling and yet feeling very overwhelmed by the sweetness that she was exhibiting I said, "You'll get better."

She shook her head and to this negativity I responded by leaning forward to press my lips in against her ear in a wet kiss. She shivered in my grasp even as I heard a moan escape through her lips.

She stood unresisting then as I continued to wetly plunge my tongue into her ear and kiss around the edges of it. Her breathing had picked up and warmly against the perfection of her ear I said, "I made something for you to help with today."

Her head turned to look at me curiously and letting go of her bottom I held something up from a nearby table. Her expressive eyes blinked and then traced to mine with a worried but accepting trepidation that kept her lips sealed against any complaint or protest.

Turning her I pressed on her shoulder and she bent down over the table before her willingly. With one hand I warmly stroked up and down upon her back and saw her relax visibly beneath my touch.

Setting the object that I had carved out of a carrot, a rather large carrot, down, I dipped my fingers into a bowl of oil and pulling the shirt she wore up I exposed her bottom and dribbled the oil from my fingers into the crack of her bottom before I then warmly pressed and rubbed upon her tight entrance hidden there with my finger.

She resisted me in nothing that I did, but meekly she remained poised for my touch upon her and as I started to make way into her with one finger she bravely breathed out and even pushed back with an utter acceptance of submission to what was happening.

My oily finger slid fully to the hilt within her and I heard her gasp slightly. Then for a moment her bottom tightly constricted about my finger as her control to be freely open for me evaporated.

"Easy now." I soothed out on a rumble of breath as with my free hand I rubbed her spine consolingly.

The tight strain of her ass about my finger eased as did her breathing.

Slowly, she turned her face to the side and lay her cheek on the table even as I felt her surrender to me even further.

I withdrew my finger only to begin working two of my fingers into her. Meekly she remained as she was as both of my oiled fingers eventually sank all the way to the hilt within her unbelievably tight ass.

I left them there for a long moment and then I pulled them free slowly. Picking up the carrot I twirled it about in the oil and bringing the blunted off end of it to the contracting door of her bottom I slowly began pushing it in as I rubbed her back reassuringly.

Her hands closed into fists upon the table but she said nothing as I saw her valiantly work on breathing and releasing her bottom by pushing out against the invasion of it that was occurring.

The shortened but quite thick carrot slid fully inside only to stop as it became seated against her entrance by the indent that I had carved into it.

Taking my oily fingers I rubbed them massaging over both cheeks of her rear as well as the top of her thighs for several long moments.

Removing my hand I let my shirt that she wore as a dress fall down over her now beautifully pierced rear.

I gently pulled her up and turned her about then. Her eyes were wide and she looked unsettled, even emotional.

It was obvious that the moment for her was a very awkward one. I said nothing other than to simply begin kissing her and then softly she began to kiss me in return until I felt the tension within her body abate some even as it grew more accepting of the thick diameter of the carrot that was dilating her ass in preparation for my later possession of it with my even thicker cock.

Moving her around the table I made her to sit down and she did so rigidly. As she sat at the table I made a new omelet and when it was ready I sat down and fed her mouthful after mouthful of the omelet until she was full.

"I'm going for a walk. Would you care to accompany me?"

She blinked intensely for a moment but sat there in silence.

I rose up and made to walk away.

"Yes!"

I turned back to her.

Emotionally she whispered, "Yes, I'll go with you."

Smiling, I said, "Good. Now before we go I want you to take off my shirt."

Blushing she rose up from the table and then meekly did as I had ordered.

Standing there naked she shyly folded her arms over top of her breasts, only making her look more desirable to me by doing so.

I let her hide them for the moment from me. Grasping her elbow I pulled her toward the door.

Walking stiffly she acquiesced and going to the door we stepped out into the warm sunlight of the morning. It was clearly going to be a beautiful day and I led her about nowhere in particular.

Gradually her crossed arms fell and when they did I captured her hand. We were walking barefoot through the black dirt of one of the gardens when for the first time she spoke.

At the moment she was gazing at a patch of carrots and darkly I heard her utter, "I may never eat a carrot again for the rest of my life."

Throwing my head back I laughed.

Looking at her then in all her naked splendor as she stood beside me in the glory of a sunny morning I shook my head with humor at her.

Gazing into her eyes I soberly said, "I can pull it out if you want."

"Please do."

Keeping my gaze locked on hers I said, "When it comes out my cock goes in."

Her eyes didn't blink as she softly responded with, "I know."

Leaning forward I kissed her and her lips warmly responded to mine. She was ready.

Turning her away from me I pushed on her shoulders and together we made our way down to our knees in the warm black dirt of the garden. Gently I leaned forward and slowly bit my teeth into her neck and as I did her whole body shivered convulsively.

Letting go of her neck I pushed with a hand to her upper back until her breath was full of the essence of the earth, even as her breasts were made to conform into it. I watched as her fingers curled into the black dirt of the garden even as I beheld her perfectly proportioned rear displayed before me ripe for the taking.

The thick carrot was not the focus of my attention though. Coming close I spread her thighs wider in the dirt and with a firm grip upon her wide hips I began easing my aching cock into the soaked wetness that was her womanhood.

Gasping as my cock eased into her she turned her face back to me and huffed out, "I.... I thought......"

"I make the rules Olivia, understand? And if I choose to alter them what is it to you."

"Yes." She breathed out shakily with and then almost under her breath I heard her whisper, "Master."

I gave her the rest of my shaft.

Her wondrous femininity clamped about me with a gloriously wet snugness even as her fist hit the ground of the garden in a release of force that said she was experiencing an orgasm by the simple act of having been penetrated by me for the first time.

In effect, she was reaping the effects of being doubly gored by two aspects of size that she'd never experienced before.

I surged back and forth deeply within her willing sheath even as she cried out and clawed at the ground like a lioness fiercely wanting everything she was getting. There was no way presented with the aspect of having his beautiful woman displayed here on her knees before me eagerly accepting my cock all the way into her womanhood that was going to allow me to last more than even a few minutes.

Still I fought to maintain control until once more I felt the orgasmic grip of her about my shaft in clear evidence of how overwhelmed with pleasure she had become. In that moment I let go and slamming forward into her as deeply as I could go, I let her have my seed. All of it.

Breathing heavy I stared heavenward and fought to not be overwhelmed by how powerful my own orgasm was.

Gradually as I remained pressed to the hilt within her I felt myself come back to the plane of existence that I existed in.

Opening my eyes I gazed down upon the beauty of our joining. She was mine now.

Leaning forward over her back I heard her ragged breathing break apart in a gasp as my still rock hard shaft put even more pressure upon the gates of her womb.

Feeling primal and savage I asked, as my large hands gripped her wide hips hard enough to bruise, "Who is your, Master?"

Her head now lay to the side on the ground and I watched as her eyes opened even as she panted heavy for breath.

"You are." She said huskily and there was no lie in her eyes.

"Of everything?"

"Yes." She whispered and then softly added, "I will serve you with everything that I am to my dying day."

All of the possessive aggression that I had been feeling stilled within me and pulling back I unseated myself from her wet clasping flesh that still rhythmically throbbed of past orgasm.

Taking a hold of the carrot's base I pulled it slowly free of her clutching ass.

Swiftly and much to her surprise then I turned her about. The front of her was stained dark from the rich dirt that I had pressed her down against and in some ways she was now a match for my darker skin color.

Breathing heavy I pushed her dirt stained knees upward and as I did I looked down upon the contracting actions of her anus that even now was soaking up the copious amounts of feminine juice and seed spilling out of her womanhood.

With her knees in the air I took my hand and depressed my shaft enough to line up with her ass until the warmly contracting actions of its entrance nuzzled around the head of my shaft.

My hands found the dirt to either side of Olivia's head even as her legs were stretched up past my shoulders.

Leaning down I licked her nipple that tasted of both her and the dirt I was originally created of, even as with a slow and steady aggression I made way into her oiled rear with my very wet cock.

I didn't stop and with eyes wide and breathe coming hard I watched Olivia as true to my word I made her take every last inch of me until there was none left to give.

Seated to the full at last within her I let her legs spill off of my shoulders even as I came down to crush her dirt stained breasts with my chest. To my surprise I felt her legs curl about my waist in an intimate hug as if to welcome the possession of all aspects of her bodily form by her mate.

Opening my eyes as I fought hard not to come straight off in the hot and incredibly soft depths of her ass I was welcomed by the feeling of her kiss on my lips.

Meeting her gaze I watched her grin and softly say, "I'll eat carrots every day if it turns into moments like this."

I heard the truth of her words even as her eyes showed me that far from experiencing any excruciating pain she was instead clearly enjoying the moment of my possession of the most sensitive part of her anatomy.

Taking her face in my hands I held it steady for my kisses even as her thighs held me pressed in deeply within her ass. I withdrew partially only to press in the whole way again and when I did I was treated to a gasp of pleasure escaping out against my lips from hers.

Moaning she begged, "Do it again!"

I did.

"Harder! Oh please, harder!"

I did as asked, until I simply couldn't hold my resurgent seed within me any longer. I let go explosively within her depths even as my eardrum was deadened by the sound of her scream of pleasure.

Her nails sank deeply into my back and breathing heavy with release I leaned forward enough to sink my teeth none to gently into the joining of her neck with her shoulder.

When I did so I was treated to the feeling of her body locking up in an orgasm so extreme that I couldn't even move my cock within her ass as she held it as deep within her as it would go with a viselike grip.

Groaning, I shuddered for truly I didn't want to be anywhere else than where I was in this moment.

Gradually the extremeness of our joining dissipated and I forced myself to slide free of her hotly clamped down ass.

Raising up in the dirt I could see that she was fast leaving the conscious world being completely spent of all energy by the orgasm still continuing to throb its way through her being in replica of something that just wouldn't die.

Tenderly I picked her up and carried her the long walk to the pool of warm water down by the river.

She awoke in my arms dreamily as I settled us both down into the water. She stroked her dirt stained cheek against my chest and dreamily asked, "Can we stay here for a while?"

"I don't have anywhere to go, do you?"

Her hand rose and stroked along my lips seductively before falling limply into the water as she whispered, "I'm where I want to be."

And then with an even more seductive quality to her voice she breathed out, "I'm with my, Master."

With that said her eyes closed and she went back to sleep in my arms.

Holding her to me I laid my own head back and rested even as I acknowledged deeply that I was exactly where I wanted to be too.

THE END

Dear Reader,

All of the more common issues put aside I find it utterly ridiculous how most of the powers that be have come together in unison to agree that men shouldn't be like themselves anymore, because it's 'toxic'. A famous male Hollywood director actually just came out and paraphrasing said, 'Testosterone is a poison that needs to be eradicated from the male side of the species.' Count me out of this modern utopia that popular culture is seeking to enforce – I'll be with the Westwilds. If you'd like to read another book that enforces the need and benefits of strong male masculinity then I suggest, *Book Mate.* A First Chapter Excerpt is on the next page. Enjoy!

Author's Corner

It would seem that the genre of Erotic Christian Fiction, which I have coined in terms of labeling what I have written, appears to be an entirely new avenue within the Fiction market. Many, who call themselves 'Christian' will not understand what I have taken upon myself to do and in general I expect reactions to what I've written to be hostile and that's okay. Why is that okay? The reason it is okay is because it is better to do what God says then stay hidden safely away within the mass of a group and only do what is perceived amongst the group as 'okay'. Truly the path to hell is paved with both the 'doctrines of man' and 'group think'. I write what I do, because I follow the leading of the Holy Spirit of God and nothing else. This avenue of Christian Erotic themed fiction is something He laid upon my heart to do and I chose to obey the calling and go wherever He wanted it to go. It is within my heart to be obedient to God always and to that end I have gone farther than I ever expected to be asked of me by my God in terms of witnessing to a lost and dying world, but even so, His will be done. If you have questions or comments, please feel free to direct them to me at the following email address: I don't always have answers, but I can pray for you and whatever I can't do – God can.

author-aedan-sayla@proton.me

Thanks for reading and please do leave a review!

Book Mate

Chapter One

The front doors swung open forcefully.

I didn't even have to look up to know who it was.

More government people no doubt.

There was a loud, "Ahem." followed by an impatient release of air.

Slowly I brought my head up to look out over the top of my glasses in my best impersonation to seem pleasant, as I took in the three men in dark suits beyond the counter. Definitely the people from the government again.

Oops, one of them was a woman. It was getting increasingly hard to tell the difference between the two these days sometimes.

Smoothing my hands over my skirt I stood up and said, "How may I be of help?"

"Mr. Fortanel is in, correct?"

Before I could speak he impatiently waved his hand and said, "But of course he is, I already know that, tell me where he is?"

Feeling anger come to life all along the edges of my hard-fought for good manners, I tightly smiled and said, "Whether he is in or not is no guarantee that you are going to see him. Do you have an appointment, if so I will be happy to show you the way."

The man, who towered over me by at least a foot, gritted his teeth together and leaned over the polished mahogany counter. I didn't budge one inch.

I watched him lean in closer and closer with an utter stillness of regard. Two more inches closer to my face and a rather fine third edition of Tom Sawyer was going to crush his incoming face with the stated resolve to do maximum damage.

I was tired of these government goons that marched in here like they owned the place!

I had quite a few in town that I would call to be my friend, but none so much as my employer, Mr. Fortanel. To me he was far more like a father than an employer and these goons along with whoever they worked for were contributing heavily to the decline in health of someone that I fiercely loved.

Proximity superseded I gripped the hardbound book with steeled resolve and flexed to throw everything I had into the hit. Lamentedly everything I had to throw wasn't all that much.

I weighed exactly 122 pounds and about 5 pounds of that had to be hair. It didn't matter, I was all in.

"D'Asia that will be quite enough!" came the weak sounding voice of my employer that sounded out just loud enough in my ear to break my focus of intent to cause bodily harm.

I froze in my actions to rearrange the face of the man that had come too far into my personal space.

Breathing out with a loud sigh I set the hardback book back down upon the desk.

"Really dear, that would've been too hard on the book. A face like that could split granite for lack of any perceivable intelligence."

I touched the earbud next to my ear and said, "You're sure, Mr. Fortanel? I can send them away."

"No, no, my dear. I'm afraid they'd only come back with beefier women. My eyes are failing me, as you know, but that one on the left is indeed a woman, correct?"

Not being able to help myself I confirmed with a smile, "Yes, Sir."

"Send them up."

The smile fell from my face as I reengaged with the man who had pulled back over to his side of the countertop. His face wore a shocked expression as his gaze went from me to the book lying on the counter near my fingers.

Coldly, I said, "Mr. Fortanel will see you now. Take the elevator. Third-floor office that overlooks the gallery."

All three looked upward in the expansive gallery that opened up all around the front desk till their gazes rose three stories up to where an old man was visible sitting at his chair before an enormous desk. Sullenly the three retreated from me to go to the clear-sided crystalline looking elevator that sat at the corner of the gallery.

Silent library onlookers viewed the scene in silence not knowing for sure what was going on. In that, I was also like them, I didn't really know what was going on either.

Three weeks ago a steady stream of visitors had begun arriving at the library from the government to speak with Mr. Fortanel. Several times arguments had broken out and twice I'd had to call security.

Speaking of which - I engaged the private intercom system with a finger and spoke, "Jimmy, we have more visitors, if you know what I mean."

"Got it. I'll come take a look." He responded back with quickly.

I did the tasks before me at the counter almost remotely as all of my attention was focused on what I could see of the three individuals now entering my employer's office three stories up above my head in the gabled off gallery portion of the library.

I abruptly gasped, as seemingly without any word spoken, the leader of the three ordered his two accomplices to go behind the desk and seize a hold of Mr. Fortanel.

They began forcibly dragging him from the room. I jammed the intercom button, "Jimmy get here now!!!"

In the next instant my phone was up and I was dialing 911.

Concisely I explained that an assault was taking place along with the location before I was up on my feet and dropping the phone onto the front desk.

Running across the marble tiles in my high heels I steeled myself to do far worse than I'd been willing to do before to the three invaders of this quiet library realm.

Because of the press of bodies in the clear sided elevator I could not see Mr. Fortanel and then the doors of the elevator were opening and the man from the counter was trying to grab at me as I rushed forward. Smoothly I reached forward to grab him instead, only to pull him towards me in a jujitsu move.

I pivoted away at the last moment and the man twice my body weight went crashing hard to the marble floor. Ready to kill if needed I swung around to face the other two, who I saw were instead rising from up off their knees even as they had uncertain looks upon their thuggish faces as to what to do next.

There on the floor at their feet was Mr. Fortanel!

His eyes were barely open and he was gasping weakly for breath.

His head turned to me and one of his arms flapped out towards me. Diving forward to my knees beside him I grabbed up his hand and gripped it tightly.

His eyes were moving around unsteadily and desperately I cried out, "Mr. Fortanel?", as tears spilled their way down my cheeks in abandon.

His head rolled my way and he mouthed out something unintelligible before briefly gripping at my hand and then he was gone from consciousness. I thought that he had died for a moment, but as I pressed my finger to his neck I still felt a weak pulse.

Sirens sounded from outside and the hired government lackeys suddenly looked the part of wanting nothing more to do with the situation. They hurriedly moved for the main entrance intent to escape the scene that had drawn everyone's attention in the library.

Jimmy came rolling to a stop just ahead of them, "Hey! What's going on here?"

Without a word the female of the three grabbed Jimmy and in two short seconds he was laid out unconscious upon the floor. The three then burst through the front doors and were going down the steps outside completely unimpeded by anyone.

A squad car pulled up and two cops jumped out with guns clearing the holsters. In response the three simply pulled back their coats to reveal badges and in consternation of not knowing what to do in the moment the three government goons made the most of it and hopped in their car and fled the scene with the cops looking on.

Looking up at the bystanders in the entry gallery I hysterically cried out, "Someone call an ambulance!"

Everything after that went sort of gray in the hours that followed. During which time I stayed by his side as much as possible.

The ambulance came and I followed behind it once Mr. Fortanel was loaded. At the hospital everything became a flurry of action as he was whisked away by doctors.

I was pointed to a waiting room and there I sat down. I waited for hours and hours and finally the door came open and I rose quickly to face the surgeon before me.

He looked me over doubtfully as he asked, "Are you his family?"

Some prejudices die hard in a southern community and being made once more aware of my dark skin and wildly flowing kinky hair I said, "No, he's my employer."

"Does he have any family?"

"He has a son, but he's not in the country at the moment. I....how is he?"

The doctor hesitated for a moment before saying, "Not good. We've done our best and for the moment he seems stable. He's in a coma though and quite frankly I don't look for him to pull out of it. A number of systems are not functioning as they should."

Nodding I said, as tears flowed down my face, "Can I see him?"

The doctor hesitated a little less this time before turning to lead me down the hall behind him. Entering the room I went to the side of the bed as various life-sustaining machines whirled and beeped away to either side of the bed.

Grasping his hand laying on the cover I shivered inwardly with the experience of feeling how cold it felt to the touch. I wrapped both of my hands about his willing if I could for his body to come back to full life.

Looking up I asked, "How long do you think he has?"

The doctor quietly shook his head before saying, "It could be hours, days maybe, even a week, but I...... I don't look for any kind of long-term recovery."

I nodded emotionally and stood there for a long moment saying nothing.

Inwardly, I prayed away passionately and when I was done I leaned down to kiss the ashened complexion of my employer's forehead.

Though I had several good friends I had no family. No family except for this man, who had taken me in at the age of 14 and given me an illegal under the counter job.

A job that he had always paid me three times over what it was worth.

When I turned 16 he had outright hired me on the spot. He'd even given me a place to stay in the back of the Library and from that day forward the Library and its workings had become my life.

I had never attended college, although Mr. Fortanel would have gladly paid for it, but instead he said that college for the most part was a joke and that a real education was to be had right there in the Library.

Heeding his advice I had read and read, and along with his tutoring I had become something of an expert in many fields of scope over the last ten years of my life.

The man lying so still and barely alive on the bed was the one who had literally opened up the entire world for me. I didn't know what to do now and it seemed in the moment that my life, which I had come to love, was coming to an end with the passing of this man.

"He should be left to rest now."

I nodded and let go of his hand.

"Do you mind if I come back?"

"I....normally it's just supposed to be family, but....you're welcome anytime."

"Thank you!" I whispered before hurrying from the room.

Before I left the hospital I went to check up on Jimmy who'd also been brought along to the hospital. He was going to be fine.

Forcing myself to move on with life I went back to my car.

Anxiously I hurried back to the ornately gilded library situated on a hill overlooking the town below.

Going in through the massive doors at the front I was met by my two assistant librarians who had done well in holding down the fort in my absence. I told them what I knew and after that they returned back to their tasks.

Shakily, I let myself collapse down into my chair behind the front desk. Even though I felt completely worn out my mind feverishly went back and forth over everything again and again.

The imagery of Mr. Fortanel laying on the elevator floor.

Diving to my knees to be by his side.

Taking his hand.

The short moment of clarity as he'd recognized me and tried to speak.

The words had been unintelligible, but I had read his lips.

What he'd said was, "*Don't let them change the seasons!*"

Slowly within my mind I went over the odd phrase again and again in search of meaning. Memory of something of a similar context ignited briefly in my mind.

I got up and maneuvered my way through the richly appointed surrounds of the library. Finding the rare Bible collection I stopped.

Unlocking the case I picked up an original 1610 King James Version of the Bible and carefully flipped to Daniel 7:25. I reread what the passage said twice, even as a sensory feeling, likened to the expression of having someone walk across your grave, occurred to me.

Putting the Bible back into the case I locked it back up and slowly made my way back to the front of the library.

Regaining my seat I let myself go into the world of my thoughts and ignore all my other responsibilities.

What could Mr. Fortanel have possibly meant by speaking such ominously rooted words?

The End of Chapter One Excerpt

The rest of the story can be purchased at Amazon.com and other online eBook retailers ***OR*** *you could check in with me via email and if you agree to leave an honest review a free review eBook copy of the book may be emailed to you.*

The choice is yours – in any regard I deeply appreciate the effort to support me in my work; however, it is given.

Sincerely,

Aedan

www.ingramcontent.com/pod-product-compliance
Lightning Source LLC
LaVergne TN
LVHW090125160826
845673LV00015B/847

* 9 7 9 8 3 7 4 6 2 2 6 6 9 *